Tales From Colleton County
a Deborah Knott anthology

Margaret Maron

ISBN 978-0-9984940-3-6
Oconee Spirit Press, Waverly TN

Tales From Colleton County : a Deborah Knott anthology
Some of the stories in this book were previously published as:
"Deborah's Judgment," *A Woman's Eye*, Delacorte, 1991
"Fruitcake, Mercy, and Black-Eyed Peas," *Christmas Stalkings*, Mysterious Press, 1991
"What's a Friend For?" *Partners in Crime*, NAL, 1994
"With This Ring," *Crimes of the Heart*, Berkley Books, 1995
"Prayer for Judgment," *Shoveling Smoke: Selected Mystery Stories*, Crippen & Landru, 1997
"The Third Element," *A Confederacy of Crime*, Signet, 2000
"Mixed Blessings," *Women Before the Bench*, Berkley, 2001
"What's in a Name?" *The Mysterious Press Anniversary Anthology*. Mysterious Press, 2001
"The Dog That Didn't Bark," *Ellery Queen's Mystery Magazine*, December 2002
"Bewreathed," *Murder Most Crafty*, Berkely Publishing Group, 2005
"By a Hair," *Ellery Queen Mystery Magazine, January/February 2020*

Library of Congress Cataloging-in-Publication Data
Maron, Margaret.
Tales from Colleton County: a Deborah Knott anthology/ Margaret Maron
1. Knott, Deborah (Fictitious character)-Fiction. 2. Women judges-Fiction. 3. North Carolina-Fiction.

10 9 8 7 6 5 4 3 2 1
Printed and bound in the United States. The text paper is SFI certified. The Sustainable Forestry Initiative® program promotes sustainable forest management.
Cover design by Dead Center Graphics

Contents

Deborah Knott was created when Sara Paretsky asked me to submit a story for an anthology she was editing. My first novels had been set in New York and I had been wanting to bring my writing home to North Carolina. Sara's invitation gave me the push I needed to test drive a new character.

DEBORAH'S JUDGMENT

"And Deborah judged *Israel at that time."*

An inaudible ripple of cognizance swept through the congregation as the pastor of Bethel Baptist Church paused in his reading of the text and beamed down at us.

I was seated on the aisle near the front of the church and when Barry Blackman's eyes met mine, smile on my face, then tilted my head in ladylike acknowledgement of the pretty compliment he was paying me by his choice of subject for this morning's sermon. A nice man but hardly Christianity's most original preacher. I'd announced particular text and my response had become almost automatic.

He lowered his eyes to the huge Bible and continued to read aloud, *"And she dwelt under the palm tree of Deborah, between Ramah and Bethel in Mount Ephraim; and the children of Israel came up to her for judgment."*

From your mouth to God's ear, Barry, I thought.

Eight years of courtroom experience let me listen to the sermon with an outward show of close attention while inwardly my mind jumped on and off a dozen trains of thought. I wondered, without really caring, if Barry was still the terrific kisser he'd been the summer after ninth grade when we both drove tractors for my oldest brother during tobacco-barning season.

There was an S-curve between the barns and the back fields where the lane dipped past a stream and cut through a stand of tulip poplars and sweetgum trees. Our timing wasn't good enough to hit every trip; but at least two or three times a day, it'd work out that we passed each other there in the shady coolness, one on the way out to the field with empty drags, the other headed back to the barn with drags full of heavy green tobacco leaves.

Nobody seemed to notice that I occasionally returned to the barn more flushed beneath the bill of my baseball cap than even the August sun would merit, although I did have to endure some teasing one day when a smear of tobacco tar appeared on my pink tee shirt right over my left breast. "Looks like somebody tried to grab a handful," my sister-in-law grinned.

I muttered something about the tractor's tar-gummy steering wheel; but I changed shirts at lunch time and for the rest of the summer I wore the darkest tee shirts in my dresser drawer.

Now Barry Blackman was a preacher man running to fat, the father of two little boys and a new baby girl, while Deborah Knott was a still-single attorney running for a seat on the court bench, a seat being vacated against his will by old Harrison Hobart, who occasionally fell asleep these days while charging his own juries.

As Barry drew parallels between Old Testament Israel and modern Colleton County, I plotted election strategy. After the service, I'd do a little schmoozing among the congregation—

Strike *schmoozing*, my subconscious stipulated sternly, and I was stricken myself to realize that Lev Schuster's Yiddish phrases continued to infect my vocabulary. Here in rural North Carolina, schmoozing's still called socializing and I'd better not forget it before the primary. I pushed away errant thoughts of Lev and concentrated on lunch at Beulah's. For that matter, where *was* Beulah and why weren't she and J.C. seated there beside me?

Beulah had been my mother's dearest friend, and her daughter-in-law, Helen, is president of the local chapter of Mothers Against Drunk Driving. They were sponsoring a meet-the-candidates reception at four o'clock in the fellowship hall of a nearby Presbyterian church and five of the six men running for Hobart's seat would be there, too. (The sixth was finishing up the community service old Hobart had imposed in lieu of a fine for driving while impaired, but he really didn't expect to win many MADD votes anyhow.)

Barry's sermon drew to an end just a hair short of equating a vote for Deborah Knott as a vote for Jesus Christ. The piano swung into the opening chords of "Just As I Am" and the congregation stood to sing all five verses. Happily, no one accepted the hymn's invitation to be saved that morning and after a short closing prayer, we were dismissed.

I'm not a member at Bethel, but I'd been a frequent visitor from the month I was born; so I got lots of hugs and howdies and promises of loyal support when the primary rolled around. I hugged and howdied right back and thanked them kindly, all the time edging toward my car.

It was starting to bother me that neither Beulah nor J.C. had come to church. Then Miss Callie Ogburn hailed me from the side door, talking sixty to the yard as she bustled across the grass.

"Beulah called me up first thing this morning and said tell you about J.C. and for you to come on anyhow. She phoned all over creation last night trying to let you know she's still expecting you to come for dinner."

That explained all those abortive clicks on my answering machine. Beulah was another of my parents' generation who wouldn't talk to a tape. I waited till Miss Callie ran out of breath, then asked her what it was Beulah wanted to tell me about J.C.

"He fell off the tractor and broke his leg yesterday and he's not used to the crutches yet so Beulah didn't feel like she ought to leave him this morning. You know how she spoils him."

I did. J.C. was Beulah's older brother and he'd lived with her and her husband Sam almost from the day they were married more than forty years ago. J.C. was a born bachelor and except for the war years when he worked as a carpenter's helper at an air base over in Goldsboro, he'd never had much ambition beyond helping Sam farm. Sam always said J.C. wasn't much of a leader but he was a damn good follower and earned every penny of his share of the crop profits.

Although I'd called them Cousin Beulah and Cousin Sam till I was old enough to drop the courtesy title, strictly speaking, only Sam Johnson was blood kin. But Beulah and my mother had been close friends since childhood, and Beulah's two children fit into the age spaces around my older brothers, which was why we'd spent so many Sundays at Bethel Baptist.

When Sam died seven or eight years ago, Sammy Junior took over and J.C. still helped out even though he'd slowed down right much. At least, J.C. called it right much. I could only hope I'd feel like working half-days on a tractor when I reached seventy-two.

Five minutes after saying goodbye to Miss Callie, I was turning off the paved road into the sandy lane that ran past the Johnson home place. The doors there were closed and none of their three cars were in the yard, but Helen's Methodist and I'd heard Beulah mention the long-winded new preacher at her daughter-in-law's church.

Helen and Sammy Junior had remodeled and painted the shabby old two-story wooden farmhouse after old Mrs. Johnson died and it was a handsome place these days: gleaming white aluminum siding and dark blue shutters, sitting in a shady grove of hundred-year-old white oaks. Beulah's brick house—even after forty years, everyone in the family still calls it the "new house"—was on further down the lane and couldn't be seen from the road or the home place.

My car topped the low ridge that gave both generations their privacy, then swooped down toward a sluggish creek that had been dredged out into a nice-sized irrigation pond beyond the house. As newlyweds, Sam and Beulah had planted pecans on each side of the lane and mature nut trees now met in a tall arch.

The house itself was rooted in its own grove of pecans and oaks, with underplantings of dogwoods, crepe myrtles, redbud and flowering pears. Pink and white azaleas lined the foundation all around. On this warm day in late April, the place was a color illustration out of *Southern Living*. I pulled up under a chinaball tree by the back porch and tapped my horn, expecting to see Beulah appear at the screen door with her hands full of biscuit dough and an ample print apron protecting her Sunday dress against flour smudges.

A smell of burning paper registered oddly as I stepped from the car. It wasn't cool enough for a fire and no one on this farm would break the fourth commandment by burning trash on the Sabbath.

There was no sign of Beulah when I crossed the wide planks of the wooden porch and called through the screen, but the kitchen was redolent of baking ham. J.C.'s old hound dog crawled out from under the back steps and wagged his tail at me hopefully. The screen door was unhooked and the inner door stood wide.

"Beulah?" I called again. "J.C.?"

No answer. Yet her Buick and J.C.'s Ford pickup were both parked under the barn shelter at the rear of the yard.

The kitchen, dining room and den ran together in one large L-shaped space and when a quick glance into the formal, seldom-used living room revealed no one there either, I crossed to the stairs in the center hall. Through an open door at the far end of the hall, I could see into Donna Sue's old bedroom, now the guest room.

The covers on the guest bed had been straightened, but the spread was folded down neatly and pillows were piled on top of the rumpled quilt as if J.C. had rested there after Beulah made the bed. He wouldn't be able to use the stairs until his leg mended, so he'd probably moved in here for the duration. A stack of *Field and Stream* magazines and an open pack of his menthol cigarettes on the nightstand supported my hypothesis.

The house remained silent as I mounted the stairs.

"Anybody home?"

Beulah's bedroom was deserted and as immaculate as downstairs except for the desk. She and Sam had devoted a corner of their bedroom to the paperwork connected with the farm. Although Sammy Junior did most of the farm records now on a computer over at his house, Beulah had kept the oak desk. One of my own document binders lay on its otherwise bare top. I'd drawn up her new will less than a month ago and had brought it out to her myself in this very same binder. I lifted the cover. The holographic distribution of small personal keepsakes she had insisted on was still there, but the will itself was missing.

For the first time since I'd entered this quiet house, I felt a small chill of foreboding.

Sammy Junior's old bedroom had been turned into a sewing room and it was as empty as the bathroom. Ditto J.C.'s. As a child I'd had the run of every room in the house except this one so I'd never entered it alone.

From the doorway, it looked like a rerun of the others: everything vacuumed and polished and tidy; but when I stepped inside, I saw that the bottom drawer of the wide mahogany dresser was open. Inside were various folders secured by brown cords, bundles of tax returns, account ledgers, bank statements, and two large flat candy boxes which I knew held old family snapshots. More papers and folders were loosely stacked on the floor beside a low footstool, as if someone had sat there to sort through the drawer and had then been interrupted before the task was finished. Beulah would never leave a clutter like that.

Thoroughly puzzled I went back down to the kitchen. The ham had been in the oven at least a half-hour too long, so I turned it off and left the door cracked. The top burners were off, but each held a pot of cooked vegetables, still quite hot. Wherever Beulah was, she hadn't been gone very long.

Year 'round, she and J.C. and Sam, too, when he was alive, loved to walk the land and if they weren't expecting company, it wasn't unusual to find them out at the pond or down in the woods. But with me invited for Sunday dinner along with Sammy Junior and Helen and their three teenagers? And with J.C.'s broken leg?

Not hardly likely, as my daddy would say.

Nevertheless, I went out to my car and blew the horn long and loud.

Buster, the old hound, nuzzled my hand as I stood beside the car indecisively. And that was another thing. If J.C. were out stumping across the farm on crutches, Buster wouldn't be hanging around the back door. He'd be right out there with J.C.

It didn't make sense, yet if there's one thing the law has taught me, it's that it doesn't pay to formulate a theory without all the facts. I headed back inside to phone and see if Helen and Sammy Junior were home yet and as I lifted the receiver from the kitchen wall, I saw something I'd missed before.

At the far end of the den, beyond the high-backed couch, the fireplace screen had been moved to one side of the hearth and there were scraps of charred paper in the grate.

I remembered the smell of burning paper that had hung in the air when I first arrived. I started toward the fireplace and now I could see the coffee table strewn with the Sunday edition of the Raleigh *News & Observer.*

As I rounded the high couch, I nearly tripped on a pair of crutches, but they barely registered, so startled was I by seeing J.C. lying there motionless, his eyes closed.

"Glory, J.C.!" I exclaimed. "You asleep? That must be some painkiller the doctor—"

I suddenly realized that the brightly-colored sheet of Sunday comics over his chest was drenched in his own bright blood.

I knelt beside the old man and clutched his callused, work-worn hand. It was still warm. His faded blue eyes opened, rolled back in his head, then focused on me.

"Deb'rah?" His voice was faint and came from far, far away. "I swear I just plumb forgot..."

He gave a long sigh and his eyes closed again.

Dwight Bryant is Detective Chief of the Colleton County Sheriff's Department. After calling the nearest rescue squad, I'd dialed his mother's phone number on the off chance that he'd be there in the neighborhood and not twenty-two miles away at Dobbs, the county seat.

Four minutes flat after I hung up the phone, I saw his Chevy pickup zoom over the crest of the lane and tear through the arch of pecan trees. He was followed by a bright purple TR and even in this ghastly situation, I had to smile at his exasperation as Miss Emily Bryant bounded from the car and hurried up the steps ahead of him.

"Damn it all, Mother, if you set the first foot inside that house, I'm gonna arrest you and I mean it!"

She turned on him, a feisty little carrot-top chihuahua facing down a sandy brown Saint Bernard. "If you think I'm going to stay out here when one of my oldest and dearest friends may be lying in there—"

"She's not, Miss Emily," I said tremulously. J.C.'s blood was under my fingernails from where I'd stanched his chest wound. "I promise you. I looked in every room."

"And under all the beds and in every closet?" She stamped her small foot imperiously on the porch floor. "I won't touch a thing, Dwight, but I've got to look."

"No." That was the law talking, not her son; and she huffed, but quit arguing.

"Okay, Deborah," said Dwight, holding the screen door open for me. "Show me."

Forty-five minutes later, we knew no more than before. The rescue squad had arrived and departed again with J.C., who was still unconscious and barely clinging to life.

Sammy Junior and Helen were nearly frantic over Beulah's disappearance and were torn between following the ambulance and staying put till there was word of her. Eventually they thought to call Donna Sue, who said she'd meet the ambulance at the hospital and stay with J.C. till they heard more.

A general APB had been issued for Beulah, but since nobody knew how she left, there wasn't much besides her physical appearance to put on the wire.

Dwight's deputies processed the den and J.C.'s room like a crime scene. After they finished, Dwight and I walked through the house with Sammy Junior and Helen; but they, too, saw nothing out of the ordinary except for the papers strewn in front of J.C.'s bedroom dresser.

Sammy Junior's impression was the same as mine. "It's like Mama was interrupted."

"Doing what?" asked Dwight.

"Probably getting Uncle J.C.'s insurance papers together for him. I said I'd take 'em over to the hospital tomorrow. In all the excitement yesterday when he broke his leg, we didn't think about 'em."

He started to leave the room, then hesitated. "Y'all find his gun?"

"Gun?" said Dwight.

Sammy Junior pointed to a pair of empty rifle brackets over the bedroom door. "That's where he keeps his .22."

Much as we'd all like to believe this is still God's country, everything peaceful and nice, most people now latch their doors at night and they do keep loaded guns around for more than rats and snakes and wild dogs.

Helen shivered and instinctively moved closer to Sammy Junior. "The back door's always open, Dwight. I'll bet you anything some burglar or rapist caught her by surprise and forced her to go with him. And then J.C. probably rared up on the couch and they shot him like you'd swat a fly."

I turned away from the pain on Sammy Junior's face and stared through the bedroom window as Dwight said, "Been too many cars down the lane and through the yard for us to find any tread marks."

Any lawyer knows how easily the lives of good decent people can be shattered, but I'll never get used to the abruptness of it. Trouble seldom comes creeping up gently, giving a person time to prepare or get out of the way. It's always the freakish bolt of lightning out of a clear blue sky, the jerk of a steering wheel, the collapse of something rock solid only a second ago.

From the window I saw puffy white clouds floating serenely over the farm. The sun shone as brightly as ever on flowering trees and new-planted corn, warming the earth for another round of seedtime and harvest. A soft wind smoothed the field where J.C. had been disking before his accident yesterday and in the distance, the pond gleamed silver-green before a stand of willows.

My eye was snagged by what looked like a red-and-white cloth several yards into the newly-disked field. Probably something Buster had pulled off the clothesline, I thought, and was suddenly aware that the others were waiting for my answer to a question I'd barely heard.

"No," I replied. "I'd have noticed another car or truck coming out of the lane. Couldn't have missed them by much, though, because the vegetables on the stove were still hot. Beulah must have turned them off just before going upstairs."

"It's a habit with her," Sammy Junior said. He had his arm around Helen and was kneading her shoulder convulsively. It would probably be bruised tomorrow, but Helen didn't seem to notice.

"Mama burned so many pots when we were kids that she got to where she wouldn't leave the kitchen without turning off the vegetables. She'd mean to come right back, but then there was always something that needed doing and you know how Mama is."

We did. We surely did. "Whatsoever thy hand findeth to do" must have been written with Beulah in mind. She always reacted impulsively and couldn't pass a dusty surface or a dirty window pane or anything out of place without cleaning it or taking it back to its rightful spot in the house.

Maybe that's why that scrap of red-and-white cloth out in the field bothered me. If I could see it, so would Beulah. She wouldn't let it lie out there ten minutes if she could help it, and it was with a need to restore some of her order that I slipped away from the others.

Downstairs, the crime scene crew had finished with the kitchen; and for lack of anything more useful to do, Miss Emily had decided that everybody'd fare better on a full stomach. She'd put bowls of vegetables on the counter, sliced the ham and set out glasses and a jug of sweet iced tea. At this returning semblance of the ordinary, Helen and Sammy Junior's three anxious teenagers obediently filled their plates and went outside under the trees to eat. Their parents and Dwight weren't enthusiastic about food at the moment, but Miss Emily bullied them into going through the motions. Even Dwight's men had to stop and fix a plate.

No one noticed as I passed through the kitchen and down the back steps, past the Johnson grandchildren who were feeding ham scraps to Buster and talking in low worried tones.

The lane cut through the yard, skirted the end of the field, then wound circuitously around the edge of the woods and on down to the pond; but the red-and-white rag lay on a beeline from the back door to the pond and I hesitated about stepping off the grass. My shoes were two-inch slingback pumps and they'd be wrecked if I walked out into the soft dirt of the newly disked field.

As I dithered, I saw that someone else had recently crossed the field on foot. A single set of tracks.

With growing horror, I remembered the red-and-white hostess aprons my Aunt Zell had sewed for all her friends last Christmas.

I ran back to my car, grabbed the sneakers I keep in the trunk and then rushed to call Dwight.

It was done strictly by the book.

Dwight's crime scene crew would later methodically photograph and measure, and take pains not to disturb a single clod till every mark Beulah had left on the soft dirt was thoroughly documented; but the rest of us hurried through the turned field, paralleling the footprints from a ten-foot distance and filled with foreboding by the steady, unwavering direction those footsteps had taken.

Beulah's apron lay about two hundred feet from the edge of the yard. She must have untied the strings and just let it fall as she walked away from it.

The rifle, though, had been deliberately pitched. We could see where she stopped, the depth of her footprints where she heaved it away from her as if it were something suddenly and terribly abhorrent.

After that, there was nothing to show that she'd hesitated a single second. Her footprints went like bullets, straight down to the pond and into the silent, silver-green water.

As with most farm ponds dredged for irrigation, the bottom dropped off steeply from the edge to discourage mosquito larvae.

"How deep is it there?" Dwight asked when we arrived breathless and panting.

"Twelve feet," said Sammy Junior. "And she never learned how to swim."

His voice didn't break, but his chest was heaving, his face got red and tears streamed from his eyes. "Why? In God's name, *why*, Dwight? Helen? Deb'rah?

You all *know* Uncle J.C. near 'bout worships Mama. And we've always teased her that J.C. stood for Jesus Christ the way she's catered to him."

It was almost dark before they found Beulah's body.

No one tolled the heavy iron bell at the home place. The old way of alerting the neighborhood to fire or death has long since been replaced by the telephone; but the reaction hasn't changed much in two hundred years.

By the time that second ambulance passed down the lane, this one on its way to the state's Medical Examiner in Chapel Hill, cars filled the yard and lined the ditchbanks on either side of the road. And there was no place in Helen's kitchen or dining room to set another plate of food. It would have taken a full roll of tin foil to cover all the casseroles, biscuits, pies, devilled eggs, and platters of fried chicken, sliced turkey and roast pork that had been brought in by shocked friends and relatives.

My Aunt Zell arrived, white-faced and grieving, the last of three adventure-some country girls who'd gone off to Goldsboro during World War II to work at the air base. I grew up on stories of those war years: how J.C. had been sent over by his and Beulah's parents to keep an eye on my mother, Beulah and Aunt Zell and protect them from the dangers of a military town, how they'd tried to fix him up with a WAC from New Jersey, the Saturday night dances, the innocent flirtations with that steady stream of young airmen who passed through the Army Air Forces Technical Training School at Seymour Johnson Field on their way to the air fields of Europe.

It wasn't till I was eighteen, the summer between high school and college, the summer Mother was dying, that I learned it hadn't all been lighthearted laughter.

We'd been sorting through a box of old black-and-white snapshots that Mother was determined to date and label before she died. Among the pictures of her or Aunt Zell or Beulah perched on the wing of a bomber or jitterbugging with anonymous, interchangeable airmen, there was one of Beulah and a young man. They had their arms around each other and there was a sweet solemnity in their faces that separated this picture from the other clowning ones.

"Who's that?" I asked, and Mother sat staring into the picture for so long that I had to ask again.

"His name was Donald," she finally replied. Then her face took on an earnest look I'd come to know that summer, the look that meant I was to be entrusted with another secret, another scrap of her personal history that she couldn't bear to take to her grave untold even though each tale began, "Now you mustn't ever repeat this, but—"

"Donald Farraday came from Norwood, Nebraska," she said. "Exactly halfway between Omaha and Lincoln on the Platte River. That's what he always said. After he shipped out, Beulah used to look at the map and lay her finger halfway between Omaha and Lincoln and make Zell and me promise that we'd come visit her."

"I thought Sam was the only one she ever dated seriously," I protested.

"Beulah was the only one *Sam* ever dated seriously," Mother said crisply. "He had his eye on her from the time she was in grade school and he and J.C. used to go hunting together. She wrote to him while he was fighting the war, but they weren't going steady or anything. And she'd have never married Sam if Donald hadn't died."

"Oh," I said, suddenly understanding the sad look that sometimes shadowed Beulah's eyes when only minutes before she and Mother and Aunt Zell might have been giggling over some Goldsboro memory.

Donald Farraday was from a Nebraska wheat farm, Mother told me, on his way to fight in Europe. Beulah met him at a jitterbug contest put on by the canteen and it'd been love at first sight. Deep and true and all-consuming. They only had sixteen days and fifteen nights together, but that was enough to know this wasn't a passing wartime romance. Their values, their dreams, everything meshed.

"And they had so much fun together. You've never seen two people laugh so much over nothing. She didn't even cry when he shipped out because she was so happy thinking about what marriage to him was going to be like after the war was over."

"How did he die?"

"We never really heard," said Mother. "She had two of the sweetest, most beautiful letters you could ever hope to read, and then nothing. That was near the end when fighting was so heavy in Italy—we knew he was in Italy though it was supposed to be secret. They weren't married so his parents would've gotten the telegram and of course, not knowing anything about Beulah, they couldn't write her."

"So what happened?"

"The war ended. We all came home, I married your daddy, Zell married James. Sam came back from the South Pacific and with Donald dead, Beulah didn't care who she married."

"Donna Sue!" I said suddenly.

"Yes," Mother agreed. "Sue for me, Donna in memory of Donald. She doesn't know about him though and don't you ever tell her." Her face was sad as she looked at the photograph in her hand of the boy and girl who'd be forever young, forever in love. "Beulah won't let us mention his name, but I know she still grieves for what might have been."

After Mother was gone, I never spoke to Beulah about what I knew. The closest I ever came was my junior year at Carolina when Jeff Creech dumped me for a psych major and I moped into the kitchen where Beulah and Aunt Zell were drinking coffee. I moaned about how my heart was broken and I couldn't go on and Beulah had smiled at me, "You'll go on, sugar. A woman's body doesn't quit just because her heart breaks."

Sudden tears had misted Aunt Zell's eyes—we Stephensons can cry over telephone commercials—and Beulah abruptly left.

"She was remembering Donald Farraday, wasn't she?" I asked.

"Sue told you about him?"

"Yes."

Aunt Zell had sighed then. "I don't believe a day goes by that she doesn't remember him."

The endurance of Beulah's grief had suddenly put Jeff Creech into perspective and I realized with a small pang that losing him probably wasn't going to blight the rest of my life.

As I put my arms around Aunt Zell, I thought of her loss: Mother gone, now Beulah. Only J.C. left to remember those giddy girlhood years. At least the doctors were cautiously optimistic that he'd recover from the shooting.

"Why did she do it?" I asked.

But Aunt Zell was as perplexed as the rest of us. The house was crowded with people who'd known and loved Beulah and J.C. all their lives and few could recall a true cross word between older brother and younger sister.

"Oh, Mama'd get fussed once in a while when he'd try to keep her from doing something new," said Donna Sue.

Every wake I've ever attended, the survivors always alternate between sudden paroxysms of tears and a need to remember and retell. For all the pained bewilderment and unanswered questions that night, Beulah's wake was no different.

"Remember, Sammy, how Uncle J.C. didn't want her to buy that place at the beach?"

"He never liked change," her brother agreed. "He talked about jellyfish and sharks—"

"—and sun poisoning," Helen said with a sad smile as she refilled his glass of iced tea. "Don't forget the sun poisoning."

"Changed his tune soon enough once he got down there and the fish started biting," said a cousin as he bit into a sausage biscuit.

One of Dwight's deputies signaled me from the hallway and I left them talking about how J.C.'d tried to stop Beulah from touring England with one of her alumnae groups last year, and how he'd fretted the whole time she was gone, afraid her plane would crash into the Atlantic or be hijacked by terrorists.

"Dwight wants you back over there," said the deputy and drove me through the gathering dark, down the lane to where Beulah's house blazed with lights.

Dwight was waiting for me in the den. They'd salvaged a few scraps from the fireplace, but the ashes had been stirred with a poker and there wasn't much left to tell what had been destroyed. Maybe a handful of papers, Dwight thought. "And this. It fell behind the grate before it fully burned."

The sheet was crumpled and charred, but enough remained to see the words *Last Will and Testament of Beulah Ogburn Johnson* and the opening paragraph about revoking all earlier wills.

"You were her lawyer," said Dwight. "Why'd she burn her will?"

"I don't know," I answered, honestly puzzled. "Unless—"

"Unless what?"

"I'll have to read my copy tomorrow, but there's really not going to be much difference between what happens if she died intestate and—" I interrupted myself, remembering. "In fact, if J.C. dies, it'll be exactly the same, Dwight. Sammy Junior and Donna Sue still split everything."

"And if he lives?"

"If this were still a valid instrument," I said, choosing my words carefully, "J.C. would have a lifetime right to this house and Beulah's share of the farm income, with everything divided equally between her two children when he died; without the will, he's not legally entitled to stay the night."

"They'd never turn him out."

I didn't respond and Dwight looked at me thoughtfully.

"But without the will, they could if they wanted to," he said slowly.

Dwight Bryant's six or eight years older than me, and he's known me all my life, yet I don't think he'd ever looked at me as carefully as he did that night in Beulah's den, in front of that couch soaked in her brother's blood. "And if he'd done something bad enough to make their mother shoot him and then go drown herself..."

"They could turn him out and not a single voice in the whole community would speak against it," I finished for him.

Was that what Beulah wanted? Dead or alive, she was still my client. But I wondered: when she shot J.C. and burned her will had she been of sound mind?

By next morning, people were beginning to say no. There was no sane reason for Beulah's act, they said, so it must have been a sudden burst of insanity and wasn't there a great-aunt on her daddy's side that'd been a little bit queer near the end?

J.C. regained consciousness, but he was no help.

"I was resting on the couch," he said, "and I never heard a thing till I woke up hurting and you were there, Deb'rah."

He was still weak, but fierce denial burned in his eyes when they told him that Beulah had shot him. "She never!"

"Her fingerprints are on your rifle," said Dwight.

"She never!" He gazed belligerently from Donna Sue to Sammy Junior. "She never. Not her own brother. Where is she? You better not've jailed her, Dwight!"

He went into shock when they told him Beulah was dead. Great sobbing cries of protest wracked his torn and broken body. It was pitiful to watch. Donna Sue petted and hugged him, but the nurse had to inject a sedative to calm him and she asked us to leave.

I was due in court anyhow, and afterwards there was a luncheon speech at the Jaycees and a pig-picking that evening to raise funds for the children's hospital. I fell into bed exhausted but instead of sleeping, my mind began to replay everything that had happened Sunday, scene by scene. Suddenly there was a freeze frame on the moment I discovered J.C.

Next morning, I was standing beside his hospital bed before anyone else got there.

"What was it you forgot?" I asked him.

The old man stared at me blankly. "Huh?"

"When I found you, you said, 'Deborah, I swear I plumb forgot.' Forgot what, J.C.?"

His faded blue eyes shifted to the shiny get-well balloons tethered to the foot of his bed by colorful streamers.

"I don't remember saying that," he lied.

From the hospital, I drove down to the town commons and walked along the banks of our muddy river. It was another beautiful spring day but I was harking back to Sunday morning, trying to think myself into Beulah's mind.

You're a sixty-six year-old widow, I thought. You're cooking Sunday dinner for your children and for the daughter of your dead friend. (She's running for judge, Sue. Did you ever imagine it?) And there's J.C. calling from the den about his insurance papers. So you turn off the vegetables and go upstairs and look in his drawer for the policies and you find—

What do you find that sends you back downstairs with a rifle in your hands and papers to burn? Why bother to burn anything after you've shot the person who loves you best in all the world?

And why destroy a will that would have provided that person with a dignified and independent old age? Was it because the bequest had been designated "To my beloved only brother who has always looked after me," and on this beautiful Sunday morning J.C. has suddenly stopped being beloved and has instead become someone to hurt? Maybe even to kill?

Why, why, *why?*

I shook my head impatiently. What in God's creation could J.C. have kept in that drawer that would send Beulah over the edge?

Totally baffled, I deliberately emptied my mind and sat down on one of the stone benches and looked up into a dogwood tree in full bloom. With the sun above them, the white blossoms glowed with a paschal translucence. Mother had always loved dogwoods.

Mother. Aunt Zell. Beulah.

A spring blossoming more than forty-five years ago.

I thought of dogwoods and spring love and into my emptied mind floated a single *What if?*

I didn't force it. I just sat and watched while it grew from possibility to certainty, a certainty reinforced as I recalled something Mother had mentioned about shift work at the air field.

It was such a monstrous certainty that I wanted to be dissuaded, so I went to my office and called Aunt Zell and asked her to think back to the war years.

"When you all were in Goldsboro," I said, "did you work days or nights?"

"Days, of course," she answered promptly.

The weight started to roll off my chest.

"Leastways, we three girls did," she added. "J.C. worked nights. Why?"

For a moment I thought the heaviness would smother me before I could stammer out a reason and hang up.

Sherry, my secretary, came in with some papers to sign, but I waved her away. "Bring me the phone book," I told her, "and then leave me alone unless I buzz you."

Astonishingly, it took only one call to Information to get the number I needed. He answered on the second ring and we talked for almost an hour. I told him I was a writer doing research on the old Army Air Forces technical schools.

He didn't seem to think it odd when my questions got personal.

He sounded nice.

He sounded lonely.

"You look like hell," Sherry observed when I passed through the office. "You been crying?"

"Anybody wants me, I'll be at the hospital," I said without breaking stride.

Donna Sue and Helen were sitting beside J.C.'s bed when I got there and it took every ounce of courtroom training for me not to burst out with it. Instead I made sympathetic conversation like a perfect southern lady, and when they broke down again about Beulah, I said, "You all need to get out in the spring sunshine for a few minutes. Go get something with ice in it and walk around the parking lot twice. I'll keep J.C. company till you get back."

J.C. closed his eyes as they left, but I let him have it with both barrels.

"You bastard!" I snarled. "You filthy bastard! I just got off the phone to Donald Farraday. He still lives in Norwood, Nebraska, J.C. Halfway between Omaha and Lincoln."

The old man groaned and clenched his eyes tighter.

"He didn't die. He wasn't even wounded. Except in the heart. By you." So much anger roiled up inside me, I was almost spitting my words at him.

"He wrote her every chance he got till it finally sunk in she was never going to answer. He thought she'd changed her mind, realized that she didn't really love him. And every day Beulah must have been coming home, asking if she'd gotten any mail and you only gave her Sam's letters, you rotten, no-good—"

"Sam was homefolks," J.C. burst out. "That other one, he'd have taken her 'way the hell away to Nebraska. She didn't have any business in Nebraska! Sam loved her."

"She didn't love *him,*" I snapped.

"Sure she did. Oh, it took her a bit to get over the other one, but she set-tled."

"Only because she thought Farraday was dead! You had no right, you sneak-ing, sanctimonious Pharisee! You wrecked her whole life!"

"Her life wasn't wrecked," he argued. "She had Donna Sue and Sammy Junior and the farm and—"

"If it was such a star-spangled life," I interrupted hotly, "why'd she take a gun to you the minute she knew what you'd done to her?"

The fight went out of him and he sank back into the pillow, sobbing now and holding himself where the bullet had passed through his right lung.

"Why in God's name did you keep the letters? That's what she found, wasn't it?"

Still sobbing, J.C. nodded.

"I forgot they were still there. I never opened them, and she didn't either. She said she couldn't bear to. She just put them in the grate and put a match to them and she was crying. I tried to explain about how I'd done what was best for her and all at once she had the rifle in her hands and she said she'd never forgive me, and then I reckon she shot me."

He reached out a bony hand and grasped mine. "You won't tell anyone, will you?"

I jerked my hand away as if it'd suddenly touched filth.

"Please, Deb'rah?"

"Donald Farraday has a daughter almost the same age as Donna Sue," I said. "Know what he named her, J.C.? He named her Beulah."

Dwight Bryant was waiting when I got back from court that afternoon and he followed me into my office.

"I hear you visited J.C. twice today."

"So?" I slid off my high heels. They were wickedly expensive and matched the power red of my linen suit. I waggled my stockinged toes at him, but he didn't smile.

"Judge not," he said sternly.

"Is that with an N or a K?" I parried.

"Sherry tells me you never give clients the original of their will."

"Never's a long time and Sherry may not know as much about my business as she thinks she does."

"But it *was* a copy that Beulah burned, wasn't it?"

"I'm prepared to go to court and swear it was the original if I have to. It won't be necessary though. J.C. won't contest it."

Dwight stared at me a long level moment. "Why're you doing this to him?"

I matched his stare with one about twenty degrees colder. "Not me, Dwight. Beulah."

"He swears he doesn't know why she shot him, but you know, don't you?"

I shrugged.

He hauled himself to his feet, angry and frustrated. "If you do this, Deborah, J.C.'ll have to spend the rest of his life depending on Donna Sue and Sammy Junior's good will. You don't have the right. Nobody elected you judge yet."

"Yes, they did," I said, thinking of the summer I was eighteen and how Mother had told me all her secrets so that if I ever needed her eyewitness testimony I'd have it.

And Deborah was a judge in the land.

Damn straight.

—A Woman's Eye, Delacorte 1991

This is another story that grew out of a colleague's request. Charlotte MacLeod was putting together her second Christmas anthology and asked me to send her a story. A few months after it appeared, our county's first baby of the year turned out to be the child of an unwed black teenager. Their picture appeared in the local newspaper and for several issues afterwards, every letter to the editor could have been written by either Billy Tyson or Deborah's Aunt Zell.

FRUITCAKE, MERCY, AND BLACK-EYED PEAS

Marnolla's first question after I bailed her out of jail was, "What's a revisichist?" Her second was, "Ain't you getting too old for a squinchy little shoe box like this?"

"You wanted a Cadillac ride home, you should've called James Rufus Sanders," I told her, referring to the most successful black lawyer in Colleton County, North Carolina. I switched on the heater of my admittedly small sports car against the chill December air and helped pull the seat belt across her broad hips, an expanse further broadened by her bulky winter coat. "You mean recidivist?"

"I reckon. Something like that. Miz Utley said I was one and I won't going to give her the satisfaction of asking what it was. Ain't something ugly, is it?"

"Miz Utley never talks ugly and you know it," I said as I pulled out of the courthouse parking lot and headed toward Darkside, the nearest thing Dobbs has to a purely black section. "Magistrates have to be polite to everybody, but under the habitual-offender statutes—"

"Don't give me no lawyer talk, Deb'rah," she snapped. "I wanted that, I *would've* called Mr. Sanders."

"It means this isn't the first time Billy Tyson's caught you shoplifting in his store, and this time he wants to put you under the jail, not in it," I snapped back.

She leaned back and loosened the buttons of her dark-blue coat. "Naw, you won't let him do that."

It was three days past Christmas, but she still wore a sprig of artificial holly topped by two tiny yellow plastic bells that had been dipped in gold glitter and sparkled gaily in the low winter sun.

Marnolla Faison was barely ten years older than me, yet her short black hair was almost half gray and her callused hands had worked about twenty years harder than mine. In truth our families had worked for each other more years than either of us could count and it looks like it's going to go on another generation, even though Marnolla left the farm before she was full grown.

"What in God's name made you think you could walk out with all that baby stuff?" I asked. "Two boxes of diapers? Who's had a baby now?

"Nobody," she said.

I stopped for the light and we waved to Miss Sallie Anderson, waiting to cross at the corner.

Miss Sallie motioned for Marnolla to roll down her window and she leaned in to greet us. Her white curls were covered by a fuzzy blue scarf that exuded a delicate fragrance of rose sachet and talcum. "Did y'all have a nice Christmas?"

"Yes, ma'am," we chorused. "How 'bout you?"

"Real nice." Her face was finely wrinkled like a piece of thin white tissue paper that's been crumpled around a Christmas present and then smoothed out by careful hands. "Jack and Caroline were down with their new baby, and he's the spitting image of his great-granddaddy. They named him after Jed, you know."

The driver behind us tapped his horn. Not ugly. Just letting us know the light was green and he couldn't get by with us in the middle of the lane, so if we didn't mind...

It was nobody I knew, but Miss Sallie thought he was saying hello and she waved to him abstractedly. "I better not hold y'all up," she said. "I just wanted you to tell Zell that we sure did appreciate that fruitcake. It was so moist and sweet, just the best I've had since your mother died, honey."

"I'll tell her," I promised, easing off the brake. "And that reminds me," I told Marnolla as she closed the window and we drove on. "Aunt Zell sent you a fruitcake, too."

"That's mighty nice of her. She still making them like your mama used to?"

"Far as I know."

Slyness needled Marnolla's chuckle. "No wonder Miz Sallie thought it was so good."

She always knew how to zing me.

"Never mind Aunt Zell's fruitcakes," I told her. "We were talking about you stealing baby diapers for 'nobody.' Nobody who?"

"Nobody you ever met."

Her face took on a stubborn set and I knew there was no point trying to pry a name. Didn't matter anyhow. Whoever the mother was, she wasn't the one who tried to walk out of Billy Tyson's Bigg Shopp with a brand-new layette. It isn't that Marnolla wants to steal or even means to steal; it's that her heart is bigger than her weekly paycheck from the towel factory and sometimes she gets impulsive. With her daughter Avis engrossed in a fancy job out in California and nobody of her own to provide for, she tries to mother every stray that wanders in off the road.

"What's Avis going to think when she hears about this?" I scolded.

"She ain't never going to hear," Marnolla said firmly.

Avis is a little younger than me, born when Marnolla was only fourteen. She was the first baby I'd had much to do with and I'd hung over her crib every chance I got, gently holding her tiny hands in mine, marveling over every detail, right down to the little finger on her left hand that crooked at the tip just like Marnolla's. I really mourned when Marnolla and Sid moved into Dobbs while Avis was still just a toddler. Sid split to California a few years later; and when Avis was fifteen and going through a wild stage in school, she took thirty dollars from Marnolla's purse and hitchhiked out to live with him.

Marnolla grieved over it at first, but eventually reckoned that Avis needed her daddy's stronger hand to keep her in line. Every time I saw Marnolla and remembered to ask, she had only good things to say about the way Avis had turned her life around: Avis was finishing high school; Avis was taking courses at a community college; Avis had landed a real good job doing something with computers, Marnolla wasn't quite clear what.

"Not married yet," Marnolla keeps reporting. "She's just like you, Deb'rah. Working too hard and having too much fun to bog herself down with menfolk and babies."

I'm glad Avis is doing so good, but it's too bad she can't find the time to come visit her own mother. Not that I'd ever say that to Marnolla, she being so proud of Avis and all. I can't help thinking, though, that if Marnolla had somebody she was special to, she might not keep trying to help more people than she could afford. Loneliness is a big hole that takes a lot of filling sometimes.

I pulled up and parked in front of her little shotgun, three rooms lined up one behind the other so that if you fired through the front door, the pellets would go straight out through the back screen. The wood frame house was old and needed paint, but the yard was raked and tidy and the porch railing was strung with cheerful Christmas lights. A wreath of silver tinsel hung on the door.

"I'd ask you in," Marnolla said, "but you're probably in a hurry."

"You got that right," I agreed. "I need to get up with Billy Tyson before all his Christmas spirit evaporates. Maybe I can talk him out of it one more time, but I swear, Marnolla, you can't blame him for being so ill about this after you promised on a stack of Bibles you'd never take another penny's worth from his store."

"Tell him I'm sorry," she said as she stood with the car door open. A gust of chill December wind caught the gold bells pinned to her coat and they twinkled in the afternoon sunlight. "Tell him I won't do it never again, honest."

She didn't look all that repentant to me and Billy Tyson didn't look to be all that full of Christmas spirit when I entered his office back of the cash registers at the Bigg Shopp. He gave me a sour glance and went on crunching numbers on his calculator.

"You here about Marnolla Faison?"

"Well, your ad did say bargains so good they're practically a steal."

It didn't get the grin I'd hoped for.

"Forget it, Deb'rah. I'm not dropping charges this time."

He'd gained even more weight than Marnolla over the years, and the bald spot on the top of his head had grown bigger since the first time I'd stood in his office and talked him out of prosecuting Marnolla for shoplifting.

"How come she always steals from me anyhow?" he growled. "How come she don't go to Kmart or Rose's?"

"You're homefolks," I said. "She wouldn't steal from strangers."

"That's because strangers would've put her in jail the first time she tried it with them. That's what I should've done." He glared at me. "What I would've done, too, if you hadn't talked me out of it. Well, no more, missy. This time when the judge asks me if I've got anything to say, you're not going to hear me ask him to let her off with some piddly little fine. This time she gets to see the inside of a jail, if I have anything to say about it. And I will, by damn! As president of the Merchants' Association, I've got an example to set."

"And you set a fine example, Billy," I wheedled. "Everybody says so, but it's Christmas and a little baby needed a few things and—"

"Dammit, Deb'rah, you can't talk about Christmas like the Merchants' Association don't do their part. We're civic-minded as hell and we give and we give and—"

"And everybody appreciates it, too," I assured him. "But you know how Marnolla is."

"What Marnolla is a common thief and she's gonna go to jail like one! Every time she wants to act like a big shot with some poor soul, she comes in here and steals something from me to give to them."

"Oh, come on, Billy. How much did she actually try to take? Thirty dollars' worth? Forty?" I reached for my wallet, but he waved me off.

"Don't matter if it wa'n't but a nickel. It's the principle of the thing."

"Principle or not, you know she won't get more than a couple of weekends at the most."

"Not if Perry Byrd hears the case," he said shrewdly.

He had me there. Judge Perry Byrd adores the principle of things. Especially if the defendants are black or Hispanic.

"I expect you're just tired out with too much Christmas," I said. "You have a nice New Year's and we'll talk some more next week."

"You can talk all you want." He had a mule-stubborn look on his face.

"You're not gonna get around me this time."

I made a quick walk through Bigg Shopp's shoe racks before leaving just in case something nice had been marked down. There was a darling pair of green slingbacks. I didn't have a single winter thing to go with them at the moment, but Aunt Zell had made me several floral-print sundresses last summer and they'd match those dresses.

Besides, they were only $18.50.

Billy had come out of his office to help out at the express lane. I smiled at him sweetly as I gave him the shoes and a twenty. "Unless you'd rather I shopped at K mart or Rose's?"

"*Paying* customers are always welcome at Bigg Shopp," he said and handed me my change.

But at least he finally smiled. I dropped the change into the crippled children's jar beside the cash register and went out to the parking lot with a happier heart, figuring if I kept working on him, I could maybe soften him up before Marnolla's case was called.

As I put my new shoes in the trunk, I saw the fruitcake Aunt Zell had sent Marnolla.

For just a minute, I thought about running back in the store and giving it to Billy. In his mood, though, he'd probably consider it a bribe instead of a present in keeping with the holidays.

For some reason, people like to poke fun at Christmas fruitcake and joke about how there's really probably only a hundred or so in the whole United States and they just get passed around from one year to the next.

Those people never tasted Aunt Zell's.

For starters, she uses Colleton County nuts. Not those puny dried-up English walnuts you get in the grocery store, but thick, meaty pecans and rich black walnuts. She goes easy on the citron and heavy on her home-dried apples and figs. When the dark dense loaves come out of the oven in late October, the first thing Aunt Zell does, before they're even cool, is wrap them up in cheesecloth and slosh on a generous splash of what she euphemistically calls "Kezzie's special apple juice." They get basted like that every week till Christmas.

(She says my daddy hasn't run any white whiskey since Mother died and he moved back to the main farm. The applejack he brings her every fall is some private stock he's had stashed back somewhere aging all these years. Or so he tells her.)

I live in town with Aunt Zell, my mother's sister, and I'm touchy about discussing my daddy, but it *is* the best fruitcake in Colleton County and that's not idle bragging. The one time she entered it at the state fair ten years ago, they gave her a blue ribbon.

Dusk was falling when I got back to Marnolla's. The lights on her porch blinked colorfully in the twilight and the calico cat curled on the railing came over to meet me as I mounted the two steps and knocked on the door.

When Marnolla opened it, the cat twined around and through her ankles. She scooped it up and stood in the doorway stroking its sleek body.

Her own body was encased in a long woolly red robe that looked warm and Christmassy. "What'd he say?" she asked.

It was cold on the porch and I could smell hot coffee and cornbread inside. "Let's go in the kitchen and I'll tell you."

"No."

I thought she was joking. "Come on, Marnolla. I'm freezing out here."

"I let you in, you'll start asking questions and fussing," she said.

"What's to fuss about?"

"See? Asking questions already," she grumbled, but she stood aside and let me step into her living room. It was dark except for the multicolored glow of her Christmas tree. Normally the room was neat as a pin; that night, in addition to the expected clutter of opened presents at the base of the tree, there was a stack of quilts folded at the end of the couch and a pillow on top.

"You got somebody staying here?" I asked, as the cat trotted from the living room on through her bedroom and out to the kitchen.

Before she could answer, I heard someone speak to it. The next minute, a young girl stepped into view and I suddenly knew why Marnolla had tried to steal baby items.

She didn't look a day over twelve. (I later learned she was fifteen.) Except for her swollen abdomen, she was slender and delicately formed, with a childish face. But her lovely almond-shaped eyes were the eyes of a fearful adult as if she'd already seen things no child in America should have had to see.

"Her name's Lynette and she's going to be staying with me awhile," said Marnolla in a voice that warned me off any nosy questions. "Lynette this here's Miss Deborah Knott. My daddy used to sharecrop with hers."

She nodded at me shyly from the kitchen, but neither joined us nor spoke as she picked up the cat and moved out of my sight. Marnolla was giving off such odd vibes that I briefly described Billy Tyson's determination to see her in jail, handed over the fruitcake, and edged my way out the front door again.

Marnolla followed me onto the porch and shut the door. "Lynette's why you can't let them put me in jail," she said. "She's just a baby her own self and she's got nobody else, so I need to be here, Deb'rah. You hear?"

"I hear," I sighed and drove home in the darkness through side streets still festive with Santa Claus sleds and wooden reindeer, although the Rudolph spotlighted on a neighbor's roof was beginning to look a bit jaded.

Aunt Zell had made chicken pastry for dinner and she was pleased to hear Miss Sallie's pretty words about her fruitcake, but worried over Marnolla.

"Maybe Billy Tyson's right," I said as she passed the spinach salad. "Maybe it is going to take a few days in jail to get her to quit taking stuff out of his store."

"But if there's a baby coming—"

Aunt Zell paused and shook her head over a situation with no easy solutions. "I'll pray on it for you."

"That'll be nice," I said.

While I did care about Marnolla's problems, she was only one client among many, and none of them blighted my holiday season.

Court didn't sit the week between Christmas and New Year's, so we kept bankers' hours at the law office. I made duty calls on most of my brothers and their wives during the day, did some serious partying with friends over in Raleigh by night, and, since I was getting low on clean blouses and lingerie, skipped church on Sunday morning so I could sneak in a quick load of wash while Aunt Zell was out of the house.

She swears she isn't superstitious; all the same, if I want to wash clothes between new Christmas and old Christmas, she starts fussing about having to wash shrouds for a corpse in the coming year. I've tried to tell her it's only if you wash bedclothes, but she won't run the risk. Or the washer.

Rather than argue about it every year, I just wait till she's gone.

She came home from church rather put out with Billy Tyson. "I entreated him in the spirit of Christian fellowship to turn the cheek one more time and give Marnolla another chance, but he kept asking whether the laborer wasn't worthy of his hire."

I looked at her blankly.

"Well, it sort of made sense when he was saying it." She grinned and for a moment looked so like my mother that I had to hug her.

On New Year's Eve, I ran into Tracy Johnson at Fancy Footwork's year-end clearance sale. She's one of the D.A.'s sharpest assistants, tall and willowy with short blond hair and gorgeous eyes, which she downplays in court with over-sized glasses. I caught her wistfully trying on a pair of black patent pumps with four-inch stiletto heels.

Regretfully, she handed the shoes back to the clerk and slipped into a pair with low French heels. They were okay, but nothing dazzling. Tracy walked back and forth in front of the mirror and sighed. "When I was at Duke, I almost married a basketball player."

I tried to imagine life without high heels. "It might have been worth it," I said. "Most of Duke's players at least graduate, don't they?"

"Eventually. Or so they say. Wouldn't matter. Judges aren't crazy about tall women either."

Her eyes narrowed as I tried on the shoes she'd relinquished and I instantly knew I'd made a tactless mistake.

"I see Marnolla Faison's going to be back with us next week," she said sweetly. "Third-time lucky?"

Hastily, I abandoned the patent leathers. It was not a good sign that the D.A.'s office remembered Marnolla.

"Woodall plans to ask for ninety days."

Three months! My heart sank. I could only hope that Judge O'Donnell would be hearing the case.

As if she'd read my mind, Tracy gave the clerk her credit card for the low-heeled shoes and said, "Perry Byrd's due to sit then."

Layers of pink and gold clouds streaked the eastern sky as a designated driver delivered me back to the house on New Year's Day. I forget who designated him. The carload of friends that came back to Dobbs weren't all the same ones I'd left Dobbs with and I couldn't quite remember where the changeovers had come because we hit at least five parties during the night. I recall kissing Randolph Englert in Durham just as the ball dropped in Times Square, and I know Davis Reed and I had an intimate champagne breakfast with grits and red-eye gravy around 3 a.m. somewhere between Pittsboro and Chapel Hill. Further, deponent sayeth not.

I'd been asleep about four hours when the phone rang beside my bed. A smell of black-eyed peas and hog jowl had drifted up from the kitchen to worry my queasy stomach, and Billy Tyson's loud angry voice did nothing to help the throbbing in my temples.

"If this is your idea of a joke to make the Merchants' Association look shabby," he roared, "we'll just—"

Before he could complete his sentence, I heard Aunt Zell's voice in the background. "You give me that phone, Billy Tyson! I told you she had nothing to do with this baby. Deb'rah? You better come on over here, honey. I need you to help pound some sense in his head."

It took a moment till my own head quit pounding for me to realize that Aunt Zell wasn't downstairs tending to her traditional pot of black-eyed peas.

"Where are you?" I croaked.

"At the hospital, of course. The first baby was born and it's that Lynette's that's staying with Marnolla and Billy's saying they're going to disqualify it."

"Why?"

"Because it's"—her voice dropped to a whisper—"illegitimate."

"I'll be right there," I said.

Despite headache and queasy stomach, I stepped into the shower with a whistle on my lips. Sometimes God does have a sense of humor.

Every January, amid much local publicity, the Merchants' Association welcomes Dobbs's first baby of the New Year with a Santa Claus bagful of goodies: clothes and diapers from Bigg Shopp or Kmart, a case of formula or nursing bottles from our two drugstores, a pewter cup from the Jewel Chest, birth announcements from The Print Place, a nightlight from Webster's Hardware, several pounds of assorted pork sausages from the Dixie Dew Packing Company.

Integration had officially arrived in North Carolina before I was born, but I was school age before Colleton County finally agreed that separate wasn't equal and started closing down all the shabby black schools. I was driving legally before a black infant qualified as Dobbs's first baby of the year.

I had a hard time believing this was the first illegitimate first baby the stork had ever dropped on Dobbs Memorial Hospital, but this was Aunt Zell's first year as president of the Women's Auxiliary and she has a strong sense of fair play.

She'd make Billy do the right thing and then maybe I could pressure him to drop the charges against Marnolla.

"Forget it," Billy snarled. "She's not getting so much as a diaper pin from us."

We three were seated at a conference table in the Women's Auxiliary meeting room just off the main lobby. A coffee urn and some cups stood on a tray in the middle and Aunt Zell pushed a plate of her sliced fruitcake toward me. I hadn't stopped for any hair of the dog before coming over and I wondered if my stomach would find fruitcake soaked with applejack an acceptable substitute.

Billy bit into a fresh slice as if it were nothing more than dry bread. "Anyhow, what do we even know about this girl? What if she's a prostitute or a drug addict? What if the baby was born with AIDS? It could be dead in three months."

"It won't," Aunt Zell said. "I sneaked a look at her charts. Lynette tested out healthy when they worked up her blood here at our prenatal clinic."

"I don't care. The Merchants' Association stands for good Christian values, and there's no way we're going to reward immorality and sinful behavior by giving presents to an illegitimate baby."

"Why, Billy Tyson," my aunt scolded. "What if the Magi had taken that attitude about the Christ Child? Strictly speaking, by man's laws anyhow, He was illegitimate, wasn't He?"

"With all due respect Miss Zell, that's not the same as this and you know it," said Billy. "Anyhow, Mary was married to Joseph."

"But Joseph wasn't the daddy," she reminded him softly.

"Bet the *Ledger* will have fun with this." I poured myself a steaming cup of coffee and drank it thirstily. "Talk about visiting the sins of the father on the child! And then there's that motor mouth out at the radio station. Just his meat."

"Damn it, Deb'rah, the girl's not even from here!" Billy howled. "You can't tell me Lynette DiLaurenzio's a good old Colleton County name."

"Jesus wasn't from Bethlehem, either," murmured Aunt Zell.

I can quote the Bible, too, but I decided maybe it was time for a little legal Latin. Like ex post facto.

"What's that?" asked Billy.

"It means that laws can't be changed retroactively. In this case, unless you can show me where the Merchants' Association ever wrote it down that the first baby has to be born in wedlock, then I'd say no matter where Lynette DiLaurenzio is from, her baby's legally entitled to all the goods and services any first baby usually gets. And if there's too much name-calling on this, it might even slop over into a defamation of character lawsuit."

"Oh, Christ!" Billy groaned.

"Exactly," said my aunt.

As long as we had him backed to the wall, I put in another plea for Marnolla. "After all," I said, "how's it going to look when you give that girl all those things in the name of the Merchants' Association and then jail the woman who took her in?"

"Okay, okay," said Billy, who knew when he was licked. "But this time, you're paying the court costs."

Aunt Zell leaned across the table and patted his hand. "I'd be honored if you'd let me do that, Billy."

The three of us trooped upstairs to the obstetrics ward to tell Marnolla and the new mother the good news.

Lynette was asleep, so Marnolla walked down the hall with us to the nursery to peer through the glass at the brand-new baby girl. Red-faced and squalling lustily, she kicked at her pink blanket and flailed the air with her tiny hands. Billy's spontaneous smile was as foolish as Aunt Zell's, and I knew an equally foolish smile was on my own face. What is it about newborn babies? Looking over Marnolla's shoulder, I found myself remembering that long-ago wonder when she first let me hold Avis. For one smug moment I felt almost as holy as one of the Magi, figuring I'd helped smooth this little girl's welcome into the world.

Nobody had told Marnolla that the baby had won the annual derby, and her initial surprise turned to a deep frown when Billy said he'd call the newspaper and radio station and arrange for coverage of the presentation ceremony sometime that afternoon.

"It's going to be in the paper and on the radio?" she asked.

"And that's not all," I caroled. "Since it'd sound weird if people heard you were going to be punished for trying to provide some of those very same things for the baby, Billy's very kindly agreed to drop the charges." I tried not to gloat in front of him.

"No," said Marnolla.

"*No?*" asked Billy.

"What do you mean, 'No'?" I said.

"Just no. N-o, no. We don't want nothing from the Merchants' Association." Marnolla turned to Billy earnestly. "I mean, it's real nice of y'all, but let somebody else's be first baby. You were right in the first place, Billy. What I done was wrong and I'm ready to go to jail for it."

I found myself wondering if the Magi would have felt this dumbfounded if Joseph had told them thanks and all that, but he'd just as soon they keep their frankincense and myrrh.

"What about Lynette?" asked Aunt Zell. "Shouldn't she have some say in this? You're asking that young mother to give up an honor worth at least three hundred dollars."

"More like five hundred," Billy said indignantly.

For a moment, Marnolla wavered; then she drew herself up sharply. "She'll be all right without it. I'll take care of her and the baby, too. So y'all just keep those reporters away from her, you hear?"

I grabbed her by the arm. "Marnolla, I want to speak to you."

She tried to pull away, but I said, "Privately. As your lawyer."

Reluctantly, she followed me down to the Women's Auxiliary room. As soon as we were alone with the door closed, I sat her down and said, "What the devil's going on here? First you say for me to do whatever I can to keep you out of jail, and now, when the next thing to a miracle occurs, you say you *want* to go."

"I didn't say I want to," Marnolla corrected me. "I said I was ready to if that's what it takes to get people to leave Lynette alone."

"Same thing," I said, pacing up and down as if I were in a courtroom in front of the jury.

But then what she'd said finally registered and I realized it wasn't the same thing at all.

"How come you don't want Lynette's name in the paper or on the radio?" I asked.

Marnolla cut her eyes at me.

"Who don't you want to hear? The baby's daddy? Has she run away from some abusive man?"

There was a split second's hesitation, then Marnolla nodded vigorously. "You guessed it, honey. If he finds out where she's run to, he'll—"

"You lie," I said. "She's not from the county, nobody outside ever reads the *Ledger,* and WCYC barely reaches Raleigh."

As I spoke, Aunt Zell came in uninvited. That wasn't like her, but I was so exasperated with Marnolla, I barely noticed.

"Deb'rah, honey, why don't you run home and look in my closet and bring me one of those pretty new bed jackets? Get a pink one. Pink would look real nice when they take Lynette's picture with the baby, don't you think so, Marnolla?"

Marnolla had always shown respect for Aunt Zell, but nobody was going to roll over her without a fight this morning. Before she could gather a full head of steam, though, Aunt Zell advanced with fruitcake for her and a stern look at me. "Deborah?"

When she sounds out all three syllables like that, I don't usually stay to argue.

"And take a package of turnip greens out of the freezer while you're there," she called after me.

Most of my brothers married nice women and they all seem real fond of Aunt Zell, but they sure were in a rut with giving her presents. I bet there were at least a dozen bed jackets in her closet, half of them pink, and all in their original boxes. I chose a soft warm cashmere with a wide lacy collar, then went downstairs to take the turnip greens out of the freezer.

After my overindulging on rich food all through the holidays, New Year's traditional supper was always welcome: peas and greens and thin, skillet-fried cornbread.

As I passed the stove, I snitched a tender sliver from the hog jowl that flavored the black-eyed peas and gave the pot an experimental stir. There was no sound of the dime Aunt Zell always drops in. Even if you don't get the silver dime that promises true prosperity, the superstition is that more peas you eat, the more money you'll get in the new year. I hoped Marnolla'd cooked herself some. Her troubles with Billy were about to be over, yet worry gnawed at the back of my brain like a toothless hound working a bone and I couldn't think why.

When I returned to the hospital, I could tell by Marnolla's eyes that she'd been crying. Aunt Zell, too; but whatever'd been said, Marnolla had agreed to let everything go on as we'd originally planned. We fixed Lynette's hair and got her all prettied up till she really did look like a young madonna holding her baby.

Billy had rounded up the media and Aunt Zell got some of the obstetrical nurses to stand around the bed for extra interest.

My own interest was in how Marnolla and Aunt Zell between them had managed to keep everybody's attention fixed on the baby's bright future and away from the shy young mother's murky past.

As everybody was leaving, I heard Aunt Zell tell Marnolla that by the time the baby had been home a week, people would've forgotten all about the hoopla and stopped being curious. "But the baby'll still have all the presents and she and Lynette will have you."

"I sure hope you're right, Miss Zell."

I drove Marnolla home and neither of us had much to say until she was getting out of the car. Then she leaned over and patted my face and said, "Thanks, honey. I do appreciate all you did for me."

I clasped her callused hands in mine as love and pity welled up inside of me. And yes, maybe those hands had stolen when they were empty, and maybe her altruism was even tinged by a less than lofty pride—which of us can plead differently before that final bar of justice? What I couldn't forget was that those selfsame hands had once suckered my daddy's tobacco and ironed my mother's tablecloths. And I remembered them holding another baby girl thirty years ago; a baby girl whose left little finger crooked like her own.

As did the left little finger of that baby back at Dobbs Memorial.

Aunt Zell must have remembered, too. I wondered what had really happened to Avis. The lost, scared look in Lynette's eyes did not bespeak a rosy, stable childhood. Drugs? Violence? Was Avis even still alive? I couldn't ask Marnolla how her pregnant granddaughter had fetched up here in Dobbs, and I knew Aunt Zell wouldn't betray a confidence.

"I hope you cooked you some black-eyed peas," I said.

She nodded. "A great big potful while I was timing Lynette's labor pains."

"Better eat every single one of 'em," I said. "You're going to need all the money you can lay your hands on these next few years."

"Ain't that the truth!" Her tone was rueful but her smile was radiant as she gave my hand a parting squeeze. "Happy New Year, Deb'rah, and God bless you."

"You, too, Marnolla."

"Oh, He has, honey," she told me. "He already has."

—*Christmas Stalkings,* Mysterious Press 1991

A few years ago, Susan Dunlap and I realized that her series character Kiernan O'Shaugh-nessy and my Deborah Knott probably attended UNC-Chapel Hill at the same time, which led to our writing a story together in which Deborah calls on Kiernan for help with a tricky situation. Amusingly, I heard a true-story version of this from Dorothy Cannell's husband after a colleague of his was burgled. I immediately asked Dorothy if I could use it and she generously said yes.

WHAT'S A FRIEND FOR?

WITH SUSAN DUNLAP

My elderly cousin Lunette got off the plane apologizing from the moment she spotted me waiting at the tinsel-draped gate at our Raleigh-Durham airport. "Oh Deborah, honey, I'm so frigging sorry."

Even though I was now a duly-sworn district court judge, Aunt Zell still thought I had plenty of time to pick up some of the aunts, uncles and cousins coming in for Christmas from Ohio, Florida, New Orleans, or, in Lunette's case, Shady Palms, California.

Her hair was Icy Peach, her elegantly slouchy green sweatshirt had an appliquéd Rudolph with a red nose that really did light up, and her skin-tight stretch pants seemed to be fashioned from silver latex. Nevertheless, for all the holiday joy in her twice-lifted face you'd have thought it was the first day of Lent instead of the day before Christmas Eve.

Lunette's of my mother's generation. We're first cousins once removed, which, if you're into genealogy, means that she and Mother shared a set of grandparents on our Carroll side.

But whereas most of the Carrolls have stuck right here in Colleton County ever since our branch got booted out of Virginia and wound up in North

Carolina in the early 1800s, Lunette was born without a dab of tar on her heels. She became an airline stewardess in the early Fifties, married a Jewish sales exec from California, and crisscrossed the country with him for twenty years till he took early retirement and they became semi-rooted in Shady Palms, where Lunette's continued to live since his death six years ago.

The family's tried to get Lunette to come home, but she says all her friends are there, the gaming tables of Las Vegas are just a short drive away, and anyhow, she's too old to exchange blue language for blue hair or give up the Hadassah and join the Women's Missionary Union.

But she does come back for Christmas now that Jules is gone. They never had children and Lunette says, "If I'm going to have to listen to foolish old women burble on about their blippity-blip grandchildren, it might as well be kids I'm kin to. Besides, you can't get decent sweet potato pie out in California."

We made our way downstairs through the holiday throng to the baggage claim area and while we waited for the carousel to start turning, I finally grasped that Lunette was half-crying, half-cursing because her condo had been ripped off less than a week ago.

Through Aunt Zell, I'd heard most of the details when she called two days earlier to confirm what time her flight was due in. Over the phone, Aunt Zell said Lunette had sounded almost matter of fact. Half her friends have been robbed, she guessed she was overdue; she was sorry to lose Jules's wedding ring, but she'd been wearing most of the jewelry she cared about and she wasn't all that sad to be rid of the ugly pieces she'd inherited from Jules's mother. "Everybody coos over marcasite these days, but when I was a girl, it was old-lady stuff. Yuck!"

The stereo and color TV were brand new, but insurance would replace them, too. Mostly she'd seemed annoyed because the thief had left such a mess and because the local police didn't seem all that concerned.

She was still bluing the air around us with her views on the boys in blue—a prissy young mother glared at Lunette and made a point of leading her child away—when a loud bell sounded and the carousel rumbled into motion. Soon everyone was grabbing for luggage, and Lunette wasn't the only passenger with several shopping bags full of brightly wrapped presents.

"Oh, is this young lady your cousin?" asked a middle-aged black woman when she and Lunette reached for the same shiny red shopping bag. They had been seatmates on the plane. "You're a judge, I believe? Your cousin told me about your loss. Such a shame."

Loss? Loss of what? My virginity? Last year's runoff? My freedom now that I was on the bench? Or had somebody died while I wasn't looking? No time to ask Lunette because she'd trotted off after someone who'd mistaken her garment bag for his.

We finally got it all sorted out, carried everything out to my sports car, and belted ourselves in somehow without smashing anything. As I zipped through the exit lanes and pointed the car toward Raleigh, Lunette switched my radio from a country music station to a black one that was rapping up out Christmas carols with a whole new set of lyrics. I compromised by switching it off completely.

"What did that woman mean about my loss?" I asked in the ensuing silence.

"I swear, you're as hard of hearing as Jules used to be. What the hell do you think I've been trying to tell you? Last night when I was packing, I was going to wrap it up and give it to you for Christmas. And that's when I realized that that double-damned S.O.B. had taken it, too."

"The *locket?*" I was aghast. "The Carroll locket?"

Lunette's surgically smooth face almost crumpled again. "Two hundred years it's been in our family and I was the one to lose it," she mourned tearfully. "I *meant* to get the chain mended and send it to you when you won the election, but then—"

She didn't have to finish. I'd actually lost the runoff election and getting appointed was almost anticlimactic. What with one thing and another, I had forgotten that Lunette had promised to give me the Carroll locket if I ever made it to the bench.

The heavy gold octagon shaped locket was the only family treasure salvaged when our branch left Virginia. It had been passed down in the family from generation to generation, always going to the oldest son's bride until Lunette turned out to be her father's only child. There were two male Carroll cousins in her generation, but she hadn't liked either of their wives and steadfastly ignored all hints that the Carroll locket should go back to someone with the Carroll name.

More than its age and monetary worth, the locket was valued in our family because of the myths that had grown up around it. It had been pawned at least a dozen times, given as surety in exchange for fertilizer money or to meet a mortgage payment, and more than once it had been lost forever. Or so its then-owner thought. But always the locket came back, redeemed by bounteous crops or recovered through miracles.

In 1822, it had fallen into a deep well. Three months later, it was pulled up in a wooden bucket.

In 1862, Anne Carroll tucked it inside her husband's uniform when he went off to Yorktown. "It'll bring you back to me," she whispered. He fell in battle, but a Yankee soldier sent the locket home to her with his condolences, one corner of the hinged lid nicked by the minneball that had pierced the young rebel's heart.

In 1918, while a new bride frolicked on the beach with her groom, it had slipped into the sand unnoticed. Two years later, as she helped her firstborn build a sand castle, the tot's bright red tin shovel clinked against something metallic and there was the locket, a bit pitted by the salty sand but otherwise intact.

Lunette herself had lost it last March at a movie theater. Her friends found the broken chain, but the locket had completely disappeared. Yet when she undressed that night, it fell out of her bra. "And I know I shook my clothes out thoroughly," she swore. "The bloody thing's like the monkey's paw. You couldn't throw it away if you tried."

Nevertheless, she'd stowed it in her jewelry box till she could remember to get the chain mended.

Now as we took the bypass around the south side of Raleigh, she seemed disconsolate.

"It'll never come back this time," she predicted gloomily.

"Maybe the police will get lucky," I comforted her.

My words only set her off again. "Those lazy S.O.B.'s.? They didn't even want to come out because my losses were less than five thousand dollars. And when they did come, they didn't bother to try to find fingerprints. They said whoever took my things had probably already pawned them. I didn't really care till I realized the locket was gone. Hell! They didn't even question the neighbors good. Mrs. Katzner across the street said she saw somebody loading a stereo in the back of his car and she even took down the license number and gave it to me."

She rummaged in her silver shoulder bag and pulled out a crumpled slip of paper which she shoved under my nose. "See? A California state license."

I glanced at the digits and then pulled around a pickup with two dogs and a shabby looking fir tree in the back.

"Did you tell the police detectives?"

"Of course I did. Know what those brother-buckers said?" Her voice dripped sarcastic venom. "'Ma'am, the plates were probably stolen last week. Nobody rips off a house in broad daylight using his own plates.'"

She was so upset that I asked her to let me have the license number. "I'll get someone to run a check," I told her.

"Why bother? The cops are probably right, damn their eyes. Too bad Maria Vincelli died."

She lost me there. "Who?"

"Maria Vincelli. Her brother was connected. Nobody came near our building while Maria was living there. But she died four years ago and that's when we started getting ripped off."

"Connected? You mean mob connected?"

"Mob, schmob. She never really said, but he used to come once a month to visit her in one of those shiny black cars with the tinted windows so you can't ever tell how many people are inside. Everybody felt so safe."

By the time we reached Dobbs, Lunette had begun to brighten up a little. When we turned into Aunt Zell's drive, several Carroll women appeared on the veranda to welcome her back. Lunette clasped my hand. "Promise you won't say a word about it till after Christmas," she implored. "Some of those old biddies would peck my eyes out if they knew the locket's gone for good."

Jeeter and Gloria would be sympathetic, but Lib and Mary Frances had such sharp tongues that I promised I'd hold mine. Relieved, Lunette jumped out of my car, held out her arms to the advancing cousins and cooed, "Oh, you sweet things, I'm just so glad to *see* you!"

Nevertheless, while Aunt Zell pressed coffee and fruitcake on everybody, I slipped upstairs to my private quarters and called a friend in the highway patrol. In almost no time, she called back to say that she'd tracked it down and found it'd been issued to a certain Samuel James Watkins in San Diego. No report that it'd been stolen. She then called a friend of hers in San Diego who ran his name through files out there and discovered a long string of petty larcenies. Was it really going to be that simple?

I pulled out a Rand-McNally and traced the distance between Shady Palms and San Diego. An easy drive.

My finger continued another short distance up the map along the California coast and the name La Jolla jumped out at me. Probably wouldn't do a bit of good. She was probably busy. Or gone for the Christmas holidays.

Nevertheless, I flipped to the O's in my Rolodex and started dialing.

Kiernan O'Shaughnessy and I had briefly shared an apartment in Chapel Hill while we finished our degrees at Carolina. After a stint in the movies as a stunt double, she had become a private detective and we had stayed in touch.

"Did I catch you at a bad time?" I asked.

"As a matter of fact, yes," she said, sounding almost out of breath. "Fortunately, I can still do two things at once. And even if I couldn't, I'd choose talking to you. So how're things in the wilds of Colleton Country?"

"It's Christmas. Something you probably don't have to bother with out there, but relatives are flocking in here like homing pigeons to Capistrano."

"Swallows," Kiernan corrected.

"Whatever. Listen, I'm calling about my Cousin Lunette. She's on my mother's Carroll side. I need to ask a professional favor now that you're licensed. Unless you're too busy?"

"Gee, Deborah, I'd love to help but I'm really busy at the moment. I need to do some more backbends, then catch some sun on my beachfront deck. After that it'll be time to watch bronzed young men amble over the rocks or balance on their body boards out on the waves."

Before I could laugh, she said, "Actually, what I'm doing is waiting for the one thing that will make this duplex in La Jolla perfect."

"Which is?"

"A servant. I'm running an ad for a housekeeper/cook. Someone like your cousin Lunette, who'll run the house, cook great meals, and love my dog."

I laughed. "If that's your standard, forget Lunette because she's forgot every bit of raising she ever had. She hasn't lifted a mop in half a century, she uses the oven for storage, and if she took your dog out, it'd probably be to sell him."

"Then it's just as well that I've found the perfect woman. At least I think I have. Listen to this: she managed an inn for ten years, planned the menus herself, is so tidy she straightened the kitchen counter while we talked, and best of all, she speaks in monosyllables. I'll hardly know she's here."

"But—?" I asked.

"But I'd hoped for someone who could spell me with Ezra when I'm on a case," Kiernan admitted. "Mrs. Pritchard looks to be sixty-some years old. A very matronly sixty-some. I can't see her loping along the beach with an Irish Wolfhound. Still, she likes Ezra and that's what counts in the end, isn't it?"

"So you hired her? That's nice. Now, my cousin—"

"I have one more applicant to screen," Kiernan interjected smoothly. "A man. Might be interesting to have a real butler, don't you think? Remember those old Mr. Belvedere movies they used to run on Channel 5? Who was that actor? Robert Young? David Niven?"

"I really don't remember."

"Not David Niven... Clifton Webb! But unless this guy's actually a gentleman's gentleman, Mrs. Pritchard will get the job."

"I'm sure she'll do just fine." I tried not to sound impatient but she picked up on my tone and said, "So. What's the favor?"

I had barely begun to tell her about my cousin Lunette and the Carroll locket when she said "Can you hang on a minute and let me answer the doorbell? I'll just glance over this last applicant's resume and unless he's better than David Niven or Clifton Webb, he'll be on his way before he gets as far as the sofa."

She must have taken the phone with her because a moment later, I heard a male voice. "Ms. O'Shaunessy? I'm Brad Tchernak."

"You're a chef?" asked Kiernan. "I would have taken you for a linebacker instead of a cook."

"Not a professional cook, but a great one, and a great housekeeper."

I heard a "woof" and then Kiernan said, "Down, Ezra! Sorry about that Mr. Tchernak. He won't bite."

"Just Tchernak," said the man. "That's okay. I like dogs. Even dogs that can put their paws on my shoulder. Am I'm hired?"

"Not so fast," Kiernan said, "But go ahead and check out the kitchen."

Before she could follow him, I called her name as loudly as I could and she finally remembered me.

"Sorry, Deborah. This interview's a bit more complicated than I expected."

"So I gather."

"You were just about to ask me for a favor?"

"Damn straight. You've got a slimeball out there in California and he's got the Carroll locket. My locket. The one Cousin Lunette was going to give me when I won the election. You reckon you could find out where he pawned it and buy it back? I've got his name, address, and phone number. It shouldn't be hard to find a small-time thief who steals from little old ladies."

"If the locket hasn't been melted down, I'll find it," she promised.

"Just don't get sidetracked by that linebacker," I said, knowing her weakness for big well-muscled men.

It was several hours before she called back to report no success in retrieving the locket. She had broken into the address I'd given her for Samuel Watkins by way of an open second floor window—child's play for a gymnast like her. "Unfortunately the place seems to be just an accommodation address, a transfer point. His stolen goods could be in a self-storage unit anywhere in San Diego County. Or Riverside, Orange, or Imperial Counties. Your cousin's things could be scattered around the whole southwest. Sorry, Deborah."

"Look, don't worry about it," I told her, horrified to think she'd actually broken and entered, yet quite touched that she would take such a risk for me.

"Too bad we can't sic Maria Vincelli's brother on him," I said lightly.

"Who?"

I repeated cousin Lunette's speculations about her former neighbor's mob connections and I heard Kiernan laugh across the miles.

"Maybe it's not too late," she said and hung up without another word.

"You did what?" I asked sleepily when Kiernan's second call of the evening woke me around 2 a.m. Eastern Standard Time.

Incoherent with laughter (and maybe five or six glasses of California chardonnay), Kiernan described how her new butler? houseboy? dog walker?—Californians certainly do give themselves interesting Christmas presents—had recorded a message for Watkins on his answering machine. As I understood it, this Tchernak person pretended to be a Mafia hit man who resented the hell out of Watkins ripping off his old Aunt Lunette in Shady Palms.

"I'm sorry I can't take a month off and track down his whole operation," Kiernan apologized, "but if it's any consolation, we've probably put the fear of the Celestial in him." Her voice dropped several registers to a tough masculine tone with a very credible Chicago accent. "Listen up, scuzzbag, 'cause this is the voice of Christmas Present—"

"With a little luck," she said, "he'll be jumping at every shadow and wondering how much longer his kneecaps will be intact."

I had to laugh. It wasn't the Carroll locket, but it certainly was a unique Christmas present.

"Have a merry," I told her.

"I plan to," she laughed and I heard Ezra barking happily in the background.

Court reconvened on the third of January so I couldn't drive Lunette to the airport. Just as well, since it was a long exhausting session as I handed out fines and suspended sentences to those who'd celebrated the holidays not wisely, but too well. It was nearly eleven and I was ready to fall into bed when my telephone rang.

Across three thousand miles, I heard Lunette's excited voice. "It's the weirdest freaking thing you ever saw!" she cried. "I unlocked my front door and everything was piled in the middle of the living room floor—stereo, TV, my silverware, all that blinking marcasite, Jules's ring—and oh, Deborah! The locket! It's back! I'm going to send it to Dennis's son first thing tomorrow. Did I tell you? He's getting married Valentine's Day."

"Wait a minute," I protested. "You promised it to me."

"Oh, honey, I'd love to give it to you, but don't you see? The only reason it's come back is so it can go to a Carroll bride. How 'bout I send you a diamond necklace instead?"

"Diamond necklace? I didn't know you had one."

"I didn't," she giggled. "But now I have two. And a sapphire ring. And a string of pearls. Whoever brought my things back, he left a lot of extra stuff. A ruby brooch. Some gold bracelets. A—"

As my cousin rattled on like a four-year-old detailing every item in her Christmas stocking, I sighed, reached for my Rolodex, and flipped to the O's.

—A version of this story originally appeared in *Partners in Crime*, NAL, 1994

I have always been amused by bridesmaid dresses so when I read an article in our local paper about a bridesmaid ball, this story instantly took shape in my imagination.

WITH THIS RING

"Detective Bryant," **said** Dwight's voice when he finally picked up his extension at the Colleton County Sheriff's Department.

"Can you still button the pants of your Army dress uniform?" I asked.

"Say what?"

"I was out at your mother's last week." I let a hint of mischief slip into my tone. "She said that picture of you at the White House was taken only three years ago, but I reckon you've put on a few pounds since you came home and started eating regular."

As if a district court judge has nothing better to do with her time than call just to needle him about his thickening waistline, Dwight bit like a large-mouth bass suckered by some plastic feathers and shiny paint.

"Listen," he said. "I bet I can fit into my old clothes a lot better'n you could fit into yours."

I reeled him in. "It's a bet. Loser pays for the tickets."

"Wait a minute. You want to back that mule up and walk her past me again?"

"The Widdington Jaycees are putting on a charity ball for Valentine's Day," I explained. "I know you don't own a tuxedo, but—"

"You and that Chapin guy have a fight?" Dwight growled. "Or don't he know how to dance in a monkey suit?"

For the life of me, I can't understand Dwight's attitude. It's not like Kidd's the first man he's ever seen me with, and it's certainly not like he's interested in me himself. Our families have known each other five or six generations and Dwight's always treated me like he's one of my older brothers. One of my *bossy* older brothers. Unfortunately, small-town social life resembles the Ark—everything two by two; so when I need an escort and don't have one on tap, I just call Dwight, who's divorced and still unattached. By choice, he says.

Yet ever since I met Kidd Chapin down at the coast last spring, Dwight's done nothing but snipe at him. Dwight's a chief of detectives; Kidd's a game warden. Both like to hunt and fish and stomp around in the woods. Wouldn't you think they'd mesh together tight as Velcro?

Oil and vinegar.

I've decided it's a guy thing and nothing worth bothering my pretty little head with.

"Kidd has to be at a conference down in Atlanta that weekend. Look, if you don't want to come dancing and help me act the fool, fine. I'll call Davis, see if he's free that night"

Davis Reed's a good-timing, currently unmarried state representative from down east and Dwight hates his politics. (Hey, I'd never actually sleep with a Republican, but that doesn't mean I won't let one buy me dinner.)

"Act the fool how?" Dwight asked cautiously, and I knew I had him flopping in my net.

"It's a bridesmaids ball," I said. "Everybody's supposed to wear something we've worn in a wedding."

"What's so foolish about that?"

"Dwight Bryant, have you ever looked at one of those dresses?" I was torn between amusement and exasperation.

Men.

But that's not fair. Why should I badmouth men when it's women that keep putting four to eight of their best friends into some of the most ridiculous dresses known to polite society?

Was it a man that thought it'd look really darling to send us down the aisle one Christmas wearing red plaid taffeta over four-foot round hoop skirts and carrying tall white candles?

Lighted white candles that dripped wax all down the front of our skirts?

No, that was Missy Randolph.

Was it a man that put us in skintight sheaths of bright pink satin so that the bride looked like a silver spoon surrounded by six Pepto-Bismol bottles?

No, that was Portland Smith

"What about this one?" said Aunt Zell as we prowled the far end of her unheated attic where several long gowns hung like ghosts from the rafter nails, each Cinderella fantasy shrouded in a white cotton sheet. "You girls were just precious in these picture hats."

"The hats were okay," I conceded, shivering in the February chill, "though that shade of lavender made me look downright jaundiced. It was the scratchy lace mitts. My wrists itched for a week. And Katy's parasol kept poking all the ushers in the eye."

"Such a pretty garden wedding," Aunt Zell sighed as she pulled the sheet back over that gown. "Too bad they split up before the first frost. Now where's the dress you wore when Seth and Minnie married? You were cute as a June bug in it."

"That was a flower girl dress," I reminded her. "And have you ever seen a flower girl that *wasn't* cute as a June bug?"

Here in Colleton County, if a groom has a sister, she *will* be in the wedding even if she and bride despise each other. For the record, I never exactly despised any of my bothers' brides (some of the boys got married before I was even born), but scattering rose petals can get awfully tiresome after you've done it four or five times.

The attic was too chilly for lingering and I quickly narrowed my choices down to two.

The ball committee promised us prizes in various categories. If total tackiness were a category, surely the dress I'd worn in Caroline Corbett's wedding would be an automatic winner: moss green lace over a moss polyester sateen that had already started mutating toward chartreuse before the first chord of Mendelssohn was ever played. The neckline dipped so low in front that only a cluster of green chiffon roses preserved our maiden modesty. Droopy shoulder flounces were tied up with dangling sateen ribbons that had tickled my arms just enough to keep me slapping for a fly or a mosquito. Accessories included a floppy picture hat big as a cartwheel and a wicker basket filled with more chiffon roses. What finally decided me against wearing it to the ball were the tiered net petticoats that shredded pantyhose and legs indiscriminately.

Besides, the frosty air made bare-armed summer frocks look even more inane than usual. I was drawn instead to a wintery blue velvet concoction.

Janelle Mayhew's idea of Victorian began with a high, tight white lace collar, descended to pouf sleeves that had to be stuffed with tissue paper to hold their balloon shape, and was topped (or should I say bottomed?) by an enormous bustle. The white plumed fan had barely begun to molt and it ought to amuse Dwight. Besides, the dark blue velvet, bustle and all, actually flattered my sandy blonde hair and turned my blue eyes sapphire. As a thirty-something judge, maybe it'd be more dignified to go for pretty instead of comic.

More politic, too, because Janelle and Glenn Riggsbee were Widdington Jaycees and certain to be at the ball. Their restaurant has prospered over the years and they contributed to my last campaign by hosting a big reception for me out there in the country.

The old-fashioned dress had been a little on the loose side twelve years ago; now it needed a whalebone corset with power lacing. Even with a girdle, I was going to have to sit up straight all evening and remember to laugh no harder than Queen Victoria.

When Dwight came to pick me up that Saturday night, he was wearing a borrowed black tuxedo and the fuchsia sateen cummerbund and clip-on bow tie that had been dyed to match the bridesmaids' dresses when he ushered for a friend in D.C.

"Aw and I was really looking forward to your sword," I teased.

"Mama could've let out the pants," Dwight said sheepishly, "but she said she'd rather pay for the damn tickets herself than try to get that dress jacket to fit."

Before he'd write me a check for the cost of the tickets, he rousted Aunt Zell from upstairs where she and Uncle Ash were watching the news and made her swear she hadn't added a gusset of blue velvet in my side seams.

"No gloating, okay?"

"I never gloat," I told him, tucking the check away in my beaded evening bag.

He and Aunt Zell both snorted.

Widdington's about 35 minutes east of Dobbs and we drove over with Avery and Portland Brewer. Portland is Uncle Ash's sister's daughter and therefore Aunt Zell's niece by marriage, which makes us courtesy cousins. Not that a family connection is needed. We laugh at the same things and have been friends since Junior Girls class in Sunday school.

When Dwight opened the rear door of their car, she twisted around in the front seat and said, "Oh, shoot! I told Avery I just knew you were going to wear that pig-pink thing Mother made y'all buy for our wedding."

She had a winter coat draped over the droop-shouldered horror of Caroline Corbett's green lace. In Portland's case, the polyester underlining had gone past chartreuse, right on into an acid yellow. "I'm competing in the 'Most Unusual Color Combination' category," she giggled.

"Where's your hat and garden basket?"

"In the trunk," said Avery. "The brim's so wide she couldn't fit in the car."

Before the interior light went off, Portland noticed my pearl earrings. "I thought we wore red-and-blue rhinestone hoops with that dress?"

"We did. That's why Elizabeth thought you stole the ring, remember? When she caught a flash of sparkling stones in your hand?"

"She just said that to throw suspicion off herself," said Portland. "I still think she's the one who took it."

"They never did get it back, did they?" asked Avery as he waited for a pickup to pass before pulling away from the curb.

"Huh?" said Dwight.

"Oh, that's right," I remembered. "You were probably stationed in Germany when Janelle Mayhew married Glenn Riggsbee. This is the dress Portland and I and their three sisters wore in their wedding."

"All five of you?" he asked dryly. "No wonder you can still squeeze into it."

I fluttered my ostrich plume fan under his chin. "Why, Rhett, honey, you just say the sweetest thangs."

"Don't y'all pay him no nevermind," I told Portland and Avery. "He's still pouting 'cause he couldn't get into his little ol' dress uniform?"

"You said you never gloat," Dwight reminded me. "What ring?"

Avery sailed through the last stoplight in Dobbs and headed east along a back-country road. As we drove through the cold winter night, stars blazing overhead, we took turns telling Dwight about Janelle's godawful engagement ring and how it disappeared in the middle of her wedding to Glenn Riggsbee.

"It all began with Elizabeth and Nancy—Glenn's two sisters," said Portland. "Both of them wanted the ring he gave Janelle."

Dwight might not've gone to college, but he knows about Freudian complexes. "Isn't that a little unnatural?"

"We're talking greed, not Greek," I told him, "and strictly speaking, it really began with Glenn's great-uncle."

Glenn Riggsbee was named for his mother's favorite uncle, a larger than life character who ran away from home at fifteen and went wild-catting in Texas back in the twenties. Unlike most kids who go off to seek their fortunes and slink home a few years later hoping nobody'll notice their tails dragging in the mud, Great-Uncle Glenn hit a gusher before he was eighteen, married a flashy dancehall blonde before he was twenty, and lived high, wide, and handsome for the next fifty years.

He and his wife never had children, so when she died and the big money ran out, he came back to Colleton County, bought a little house next door to his niece and settled down to bossing Glenn and his sisters around like they were his own grandchildren. Portland and I never even heard of him till our good friend Janelle Mayhew started dating Glenn, but we heard plenty after that because Janelle was terrified of him.

With good reason.

True, he'd been a Daddy Warbucks to Mrs. Riggsbee and her children when he had lots of money, lavishing her with expensive treats and setting up trust funds so Glenn and his two sisters could go to college in style. And yes, he continued to be generous with the dregs of his fortune, helping Glenn buy a first car, for instance, or doling out to the girls some of his late wife's gold and silver baubles.

But in old age, he was just as opinionated and short-tempered as he'd been in his youth. Any help he gave was on his terms and any gifts he gave came with elastic strings attached. For such a renegade, he had a surprisingly wide streak of conservatism.

He had expected both of Glenn's sisters to become school teachers and to stop work once they had babies. When Elizabeth majored in accounting and had a chance to buy into a new insurance brokerage firm soon after graduation, he refused to help. Said it wasn't fitting for an unmarried woman to be in a position to boss around married men.

The same thing happened when Nancy wanted to become a minister. A woman preacher? The very concept shocked him to the core. "Be damned if I'll bankroll such blasphemy!" Somehow he found a legal loophole that let him tie up Nancy's college trust fund until she tearfully promised not to take any theology courses.

As a male, Glenn was, theoretically, free to major in whatever he wanted, but you can imagine Great-Uncle Glenn's reaction when he finally realized that Glenn planned to use his shiny new degree in restaurant management to turn an old dilapidated farmhouse into a restaurant.

"A restaurant out in the middle of the country? Stupidest damn thing I ever heard of," he snorted. "Don't expect me to help finance it."

In vain did Glenn point out that I-40 was going to dot the county with housing developments full of wage-earning commuters happy to pay someone else to fix supper.

Nor did it open Great-Uncle Glenn's wallet when he heard that Janelle was taking cooking courses at the local community college. Indeed, he took to wondering audibly if she was good enough for young Glenn. After all, what kind of trashy mama did Janelle have that wouldn't teach her own daughter how to fry chicken and make buttermilk biscuits?

While it's true that the Mayhews were even poorer than the Riggsbees, they were by no means trash and Janelle was always a hard worker. She also has lovely manners and yes-sirred and no-sirred Great-Uncle Glenn till, when Glenn said he was going to ask her to set a date, the old man went to his lockbox at Dobbs First National and gave Glenn the platinum and diamond ring he'd bought to woo his dancehall wife.

We'd never seen anything quite like it: a huge rose-cut yellow diamond surrounded by forty tapered baguette diamonds, sapphires and rubies in a ballerina mount.

"What's a ballerina mount?" asked Dwight.

"Picture a big yellow golf ball surrounded by a red, white and blue ruffle," I said.

"Sounds sort of ugly to me," he ventured.

"It was beyond ugly," Portland assured him.

"But the diamond was what they call a flawless fancy yellow and was supposed to have been insured for eighty thousand dollars," I recalled.

"Supposed to be?"

"That's why I'm sure Elizabeth took it," said Portland. "Where else did she get the money to buy a partnership?"

"Circumstantial evidence," Avery murmured. Like Portland, he's an attorney, too.

"Not entirely," she argued. "See, Dwight, Elizabeth hadn't bought in with Bob McAdams yet, but she'd been working there a couple of years and she was supposed to have written up a policy for the ring once it went from Great-Uncle Glenn's lock-box to Janelle's finger—"

"But Elizabeth assumed the Mayhews had household insurance," I said. "And since Janelle was still living at home to save money for the restaurant, Elizabeth thought that would protect it up to the wedding."

"That's what she *claimed*," said Portland, "but even if the Mayhews did have insurance, no piddly little renters' policy would ever cover an eighty-thousand-dollar ring. Uh-uh, Deb'rah. She knew there'd be hard-nosed investigators swarming all over the place if Janelle filed a claim for eighty thousand. No policy, no claim. No claim, no serious investigation."

"No policy?" asked Dwight from the darkness beside me.

"Elizabeth dated it to take effect at twelve noon, which was when the ceremony took place and when Janelle's residence would officially change from her parents' house. The last time anybody saw the ring was at eleven-thirty when Janelle stuck it in her make-up bag in the choir's robing room next to the vestibule."

I took up the tale. "And before you ask, no, nobody was seen going into that room between the time we finished dressing until after the ceremony. Miss Louisa Ferncliff directed the wedding and she was right there in the vestibule the whole time, making sure the ushers knew whether the guests were bride's side or groom's and then sending us down the aisle spaced just right. If anybody'd gone back in, she'd have seen them."

"Who was last out of the robing room?"

"Janelle and me," Portland answered. "Her sister Faye was maid of honor and I was matron of honor. Deb'rah went first, then Nancy, Elizabeth, Faye and me. The room was empty after Janelle and I went out to the vestibule and I pulled the door shut."

"So who was first back in?"

I shrugged. "All of us. There was a receiving line with the parents right after the recessional, then we all went to put on fresh lipstick for the formal pictures and that's when Janelle discovered the ring was gone."

"And the only ones in the robing room the whole time were you six?"

"Are you kidding?" said Portland. "Both mothers were in and out, as well as Miss Louisa, the photographer, the minister's wife—"

"Don't forget Omaleen Grimes," I said. "She was dating one of Glenn's ushers and she acted like that gave her a right to stick her nose in everywhere."

"But between the time Janelle took off the ring and the time she realized it was gone—?"

Portland and I had to admit it. During the crucial time, there was just us five bridesmaids, Mrs. Mayhew, Mrs. Riggsbee, and Janelle herself.

Everybody had been sweet as molasses pie, but Portland and I and seventeen-year-old Faye Mayhew had hovered protectively around Janelle because Elizabeth and Nancy still had their noses out of joint. Glenn Riggsbee was damn lucky to find someone as fine as Janelle, but in their minds—particularly Elizabeth's—their brother was marrying down. The Mayhews were too poor to own their own home, Janelle hadn't gone to college, and on top of that, she had somehow dazzled Great-Uncle Glenn into parting with the last substantial piece of jewelry in his possession.

Both sisters had been allowed to wear the ring on special occasions in the past and each had hoped that Great-Uncle Glenn would leave it to her someday: Elizabeth because she was the oldest, Nancy because she was the baby of the family and had already been given his wife's garnet necklace. No matter how nice Janelle was to them, it was all they could do to maintain a polite facade, though a stranger wouldn't have known it for all the "sugars" and "honeys" being thrown around the robing room that morning.

A moment or two before eleven-thirty, Mrs. Mayhew had set the veil on Janelle's hair. When Janelle lifted her hands to adjust it, the gaudy ring flashed in the pale January sunlight.

"Don't forget to take that ring off before you start down the aisle," said Mrs. Mayhew. "Your finger needs to be bare when Glenn puts on your wedding band."

As if in chorus, Elizabeth and Nancy both offered to hold it for her.

"That's okay," said Janelle.

She slipped the yellow diamond into the same worn gray velvet box Great-Uncle Glenn had given his wife sixty years earlier. It was so old, the domed lid no longer closed with a tight snap, but she tucked the box into her makeup bag. Her eyes met ours nervously in the mirror. "Glenn's ring! Por?"

Portland waggled her thumb and there was the wide gold wedding band that Janelle would slip onto Glenn's finger in less than an hour.

At that instant, Miss Louisa stuck her head in and hissed, "Sst! Mothers! Places!"

The clock above the mirrors said 11:31.

We'd been primping and preening since ten o'clock, so you'd think we could have sat with our hands folded quietly and discussed the weather or something, wouldn't you? Instead we all dived back into our own makeup bags, touching up mascara and lipstick, adjusting our bustles, adjusting Janelle's veil, reminding each other how to hold the white plumed fans at identical angles, then a final spritz of hairspray before Miss Louisa herded us all out into the vestibule.

Afterwards, none of us could say who had or hadn't touched which makeup bag.

But that was later, when Sheriff Poole questioned us.

At the beginning, Janelle was sure the ring must have somehow worked its way out of the loose-lidded velvet box and slipped down among her cosmetics. Then, that it must have fallen out while we all made last-minute touch-ups. Surely on the floor, beneath the dressing table, under a chair—?

Nothing.

"Somebody's taken it!" Portland said dramatically.

"Don't be silly," said Janelle, anxiously uncapping all her lipsticks, as if that ring could possibly fit inside a slender tube. Her sister Faye was down on her hands and knees searching beneath the choir robes. "We were the only ones here and..."

Her voice trailed away as she saw Portland and me staring at her new sisters-in-law.

Elizabeth and Nancy both turned beet red.

"If you think for one minute—!" Elizabeth huffed indignantly. "You can search me if you like."

"Me, too!" said Nancy.

"Don't be silly," Janelle said again.

"Girls, girls!" Miss Louisa stood in the doorway. "The photographer is waiting."

"Miss Louisa," I said. "Did anybody come in here during the ceremony?"

"No, of course not, dear. Why do you ask?"

Janelle broke in. "Miss Louisa, could you please tell the photographer we'll be right there?"

As Miss Louisa tottered away on her little high heels, Janelle twisted her brand new wedding band nervously and said, "Look, if one of you took it as a joke—"

Instant denial was on all our lips.

"It's okay if it's a joke," she continued doggedly. "Let's go out like nothing's happened, and if whoever took it will just drop it on the floor, that will be the end of it, okay?" Her voice trembled. "Just don't tell Glenn or our folks, okay? It'd spoil our wedding day. Please?"

Subdued, we promised to keep quiet.

Without looking around, Janelle swept out to the sanctuary and we trailed along after. During the next half-hour, as the photographer grouped and regrouped various components of the wedding party, Janelle managed to send each bridesmaid back to the robing room alone. Would Elizabeth fetch her lipstick? Would Nancy be a dear and find a comb? A tissue, Faye? Oh goodness, Por, she'd forgotten her blue garter!

Before she could invent a task for me, the photographer decided to take a shot of the newlyweds' hands, and Great-Uncle Glenn said, "Take me one with her engagement ring, too."

"I'll go get it," I said brightly, absolutely positive that I'd find the stupid thing back on the robing room dressing table.

Wrong.

Nor had it been dropped on the floor as Janelle suggested. I searched every square inch.

After that, a bit of discreet hell broke loose. Mrs. Riggsbee managed to keep Great-Uncle Glenn reined in till after the reception was over. Fortunately, it was only punch and wedding cake in the church's fellowship hall and as soon as the cake was cut, Janelle and Glenn pretended to leave in a shower of rice. Actually, all they did was drive over to their new apartment, change clothes and sneak back into the church robing room where Sheriff Bo Poole was questioning the rest of us.

"I'm surprised I never heard anything about this," Dwight said as we entered the outskirts of Widdington.

"They pretty much hushed it up when it was clear nobody was going to confess," said Portland. "Janelle insisted that someone had to've sneaked into the robing room while Miss Louisa was watching the ceremony because there was no way that a sister or friend could have done her that shabby."

I smoothed the plumes on my fan. "Great-Uncle Glenn was furious of course."

"But Janelle faced him down," Portland said. "She told him it was her ring and she was the one who'd been careless with it and it was her loss, not his."

"Remember his face when Elizabeth admitted that there was no insurance? I thought he was going to hit her with his walking stick."

"So what happened next?" asked Dwight.

"I think Sheriff Poole put a description on the wire, but I never heard that anything came of it," said Portland. "Great-Uncle Glenn died a few months later and when Janelle and Glenn got back from the funeral, they found the ring in their mailbox. All the little diamonds and sapphires and rubies were still there, but the big yellow diamond was gone."

"No one ever confessed?" asked Dwight.

"Not that we ever heard," we told him.

What we left unsaid was the suspicion that maybe Janelle thought Portland or I had taken the ring because after that, we were never quite as close again.

"I don't *care* what happened to it!" she stormed when Portland pressed her about the theft a few months later. "If one of y'all needed the money that bad, then that was a better use for that darned old ring than on my finger."

Portland had called me the minute she got back to Dobbs. "She thinks you or I took it."

"She probably heard about our new mink coats and all our trips to Bermuda," I said dryly.

So we dropped it after that. Janelle was still friendly with us when we saw her, but as time passed, those occasions were less frequent. She and Glenn threw themselves into the restaurant which took off like a rocket from opening day, and Portland and I were both caught up in our own careers back in Dobbs.

Anyhow, loyalties always realign when you marry outside your own crowd. Janelle had made her bed among Riggsbees and from that day forward, it was as if Elizabeth and Nancy had never acted ugly to her.

"Well, one good thing came out of it," Portland said, paralleling my thoughts. "Elizabeth was so grateful to Janelle for understanding about the insurance mix-up that they became real friends from then on."

The Widdington Jaycees were holding their ball at the new Shriners club and as Avery drove into the parking lot, laughing couples streamed toward the entrance.

Heaven knows there was plenty to laugh at. I haven't seen that much organdy, chiffon, and taffeta frou-frou since I helped judge a Little Miss Makely beauty contest last year.

Inside, the club was decorated in valentines of every size and jammed to the walls, but friends had saved space at a table for us. While Dwight and Avery went off to fight their way to the bar, lights played across the dance floor and I saw a lot of familiar faces.

And one familiar dress.

Nancy Riggsbee was much heavier now. The seams on her blue velvet had clearly been let out and her bustle rode on hips even more ample than mine, but she beamed with seeming pleasure when she spotted me and came right over.

"Deborah Knott! How you been, lady?"

We kissed air, and half-screaming to be heard above the music and talk, I said, "Where's your fan? And don't tell me Elizabeth's here in this same dress, too? And Faye?"

"No, Faye's living in Boston now and Elizabeth's little girl came home from school sick with the flu yesterday, so I'm here on her ticket. In her dress. Mine was cut up for a church pageant years ago. Mary and one of the Magi, I think. The fans went for angel wings."

So Elizabeth had porked up a bit, too, since I last saw her? Mean of me to be smug about it. To atone, I said I'd heard about her getting a church out in the country from Durham and how was she liking it after so long in Virginia?

It was too loud for small talk though, and after a few more shouted pleasantries, Dwight and Avery came back with our drinks. I introduced Dwight to Nancy, who said she was going to go find Janelle and tell her we were there.

Fortunately someone got the band to turn down their speakers about then and conversation became possible again.

"So she became a preacher after all?" Dwight asked.

I nodded. "After Great-Uncle Glenn died, the others encouraged her to go to divinity school. It was a struggle because he didn't leave much, but Janelle and Glenn pitched in. Elizabeth, too, even though she was scraping every penny to buy into the firm about then."

"Notice Nancy's ring if she comes back," Portland told him. "After the ring came home without the yellow diamond, Glenn had the diamond baguettes set into a sort of engagement ring. They gave Elizabeth the sapphires and Nancy the rubies. Janelle told me that's pretty much what they would've done anyhow if he'd left both girls the ring—sell the big stone and make two rings out of the little ones. In the end, it made three."

I was tired of that stupid ring. The band was playing a lively two-step and I wanted to shake my bustle. Despite his size, Dwight dances surprisingly well and I didn't mean to waste the music talking about something over and done with. We moved out onto the dance floor and were soon twirling with the best.

A couple of slow numbers followed, then the spotlight fell on the emcee who announced the first category of the evening: Heart and Flowers, i.e., fussiest dress. To the strains of "Here Comes the Bride," nine women glided across the dance floor, as if down an aisle, to a makeshift altar behind the emcee. The clear winner was a stiff yellow net covered with row upon row of tight little ruffles.

Amid the laughter and applause, I felt a light touch on my arm and there was Janelle smiling at Portland and me. She gave us each a hug and said to me, "Nancy said you signed up in the prettiest dress category? I'm so flattered. It *was* a beautiful wedding, wasn't it?"

She herself was wearing ice-blue satin from her sister-in-law Elizabeth's wedding. "That's the only time I was a bridesmaid," Janelle said regretfully. "I was always big as a house pregnant when everybody else was getting married."

One of the Widdington Jaycees dragged her away to help with something and she made us promise we wouldn't leave without speaking again.

The next category was My Funny Valentine for the most unusual gown and it was a tie between a Ronald McDonald clown (the bride managed a local franchise) and a gold lame jump suit (the sky-diving bride and groom were married in free fall.)

Portland didn't win the Purple Heart Award (the most unusual color actually went to a hot-pink velvet bodice, orange organza skirt and lime green sash), but she was persuaded to enter Kind Hearts and Coronets for the most accessories and won handily with her huge picture hat, arm-length lace mitts, and wicker basket full of chiffon roses.

In between, as groups of contestants were assembled for their march down the mock aisle, we danced and chatted and filled several be-doilied sandwich plates with the usual array of finger foods found at a typical wedding reception: raw vegetables and herb dip, cheese straws, cucumber sandwiches, tiny hot rolls stuffed with ham and melted pimiento cheese, salted nuts, and heart-shaped butter mints.

Despite all the laughter, wearing the dress brought back memories of Janelle and Glenn's wedding; and seeing Nancy around the room in the same garb only emphasized the feeling. I knew Portland was flashing on it, too, because she kept going back to the missing ring. Faye, Nancy or Elizabeth. Who had taken it? (Loyally, we each long since cleared the other.)

If Faye had eventually lavished money around, we'd never heard of it so the thief had to be Elizabeth or Nancy.

"Nancy's a preacher," Portland said.

"That wouldn't have mattered," I argued. "They both felt entitled to the ring. Don't forget, she came up with tuition to divinity school."

"Elizabeth helped her though. And so did Glenn and Janelle. Janelle didn't buy any new clothes for three years, till long after Elizabeth bought a partnership with Bob McAdams. Where did Elizabeth get enough money if not from pawning the ring?"

"I thought Glenn co-signed a loan with her?" said Avery.

"Yes, but—"

"You gals have gone at it all wrong," said Dwight. "From what you've told me, there's only one person who could have taken the ring without being caught or even suspected."

I hate that superior air he puts on when he's being Dick Tracy, but all of a sudden, I realized he was right.

"Who?" asked Avery.

"The woman who directed the wedding, of course."

"Miss Louisa Ferncliff?" Portland exclaimed.

Dwight lifted his glass to her. "The only person alone out in the vestibule while everyone else was taking part in the ceremony. Anybody ever take a look at her lifestyle after the wedding?"

Avery cocked his head. "You know something, ol' son? I sort of remember when she died, Ed Whitbread was the one who drew up her will and when he came over to file it at the courthouse, seems like he said he was surprised how much money she did have to leave that sorry nephew of hers down in Wilmington."

Portland was looking doubtful. "Miss *Louisa?*"

I spread my fan and drew myself up in a most judicial manner. "It's unfair to slander the name of a good woman who can no longer defend herself, but"—I used the fan to shield my voice from the rest of the table—"one thing's for sure. Miss Louisa Ferncliff directed just about every single wedding at that church for years. She sure would know that brides take off their engagement rings and leave them somewhere in the robing room, but that was the first ring really worth taking, wouldn't you say?"

"I'll be damned," said Portland. "Miss Louisa!"

She jumped up from the table. "Come on, Deb'rah! Let's go tell Janelle."

Protesting that we had no proof, I followed her around the edge of the dance floor until we found Janelle, who, as one of the ball's organizers, had just presented the Heart of Carolina prize for the most denim or gingham of bridesmaids wear.

Quickly, we maneuvered her into the lobby where it was quieter and Portland laid out Dwight's theory and my supporting logic.

Janelle was flabbergasted. "Miss Louisa stole my ring?"

"She certainly had plenty of opportunity," I said cautiously, "but I don't see how you'd ever prove it. She left everything to that sorry nephew and what he didn't sell off, he either burned or threw out."

"I don't care!" A radiance swept across Janelle's sweet face and she hugged Portland. "We never once thought of Miss Louisa. I can't wait to tell Glenn. If you could know what it means that it was her and not—"

She broke off and hugged us both again, then whirled away back into the ballroom.

"Well, I'll be blessed," said Portland, standing there with her mouth hanging open. "Not you or me after all, Deb'rah. She really did think it was one of Glenn's sisters."

"Or they could have accused her own sister," I reminded her. "For all they knew, Faye could have been the thief."

"Oh, I'm so glad Dwight finally figured it out. Let's go buy him a drink."

"You go ahead," I told her.

The band was playing a suburban version of "Hometown Honeymoon" when I caught up with Janelle.

"You and Glenn went to New York on your honeymoon, didn't you?"

Surprised, she nodded.

"Is that where you sold the diamond?"

"What?"

"The biggest diamond market in the country's right there on Forty-seventh Street. You'd have gotten better money for it there than anywhere here in North Carolina."

There was a door off to the side and Janelle pulled me through it into an empty office, the club manager's by the look of it.

"You said Miss Louisa must've taken it."

"I said she had lots of opportunity," I corrected. "You had the most though."

"That's crazy! Why would I steal my own engagement ring? It wasn't even insured."

"I think that's exactly why you did it," I said. "You're not really a thief and you wouldn't have pretended it was stolen if it meant the insurance company was going to be defrauded of eighty thousand dollars. But the ring was legally yours, you and Glenn needed money, and that was the simplest way to get it without ticking off his uncle. All you needed to do was go through that charade."

Janelle was shaking her head. *"No, no, NO!"*

"Oh, get real," I told her. "How else did you and Glenn have enough to get the restaurant off to such a good start? How'd Glenn have enough collateral to co-sign a loan for Elizabeth's partnership so quick?"

"Uncle Glenn—"

"Uncle Glenn didn't leave that kind of money. I was nosy enough to look up the records when his estate was settled even though I never put two and two together. The house went to Glenn's mom and what was split between Glenn and his sisters wouldn't have bought partnership in a hot dog stand at the fair. That's why we were so sure one of them took it."

Her eyes fell.

"It was mean of you to let Portland think you suspected us all these years."

Janelle threw up her hands in exasperation. "I didn't want to, but it was the only way I could make her quit talking about it. I was afraid if she kept on, she'd finally figure it out."

That dog-with-a-bone tenacity makes Portland a good lawyer, but it's a real pain in the neck for some of her friends and I couldn't help grinning.

"Are you going to tell her?" Janelle asked.

"And spoil the fun she and Dwight are having, thinking Miss Louisa did it?"

Janelle giggled and I had to laugh, too. "You know, I bet Miss Louisa would love it if people remembered her for pulling off a slick jewel theft."

Better than not being remembered at all, I judged, and clasped Janelle's hand. We both looked down at the circle of diamond baguettes that sparkled modestly above her wedding band.

"It really was the tackiest ring in the whole world," she said.

"Something that trashy deserved to get itself stolen," I agreed.

As we stepped back into the room a few minutes later, someone yelled, "Here she is!" and immediately pushed me into the final lineup of the evening. Queen of Hearts. The prettiest dress of weddings past.

Nancy, in her sister's dress, had entered this category, too, and there was a truly gorgeous Scarlett O'Hara confection of pale green organza plus a couple of sophisticated black silks, but none of them had a fan of white ostrich plumes and none of them were as shameless at working a crowd.

The prize was a five-pound, red satin, heart-shaped box of chocolates.

I won by a landslide.

— *Crimes of the Heart*, Berkley Books, 1995

Chronologically, this story takes place between Up Jumps the Devil *and* Killer Market, *long before Deborah had any romantic interest in Dwight Bryant.*

PRAYER FOR JUDGMENT

Certain smells take you back in time as quickly as any period song. One whiff of *Evening in Paris* and I am a child again, watching my mother get dressed up. The smell of woodsmoke, bacon, newly turned dirt, a damp kitten, shoe polish, Krispy Kreme doughnuts—each evokes anew its own long sequence of memories... like gardenias on a summer night.

The late June evening was so hot and humid, and the air was so still, that the heavy fragrance of gardenias was held close to the earth like layers of sweet-scented chiffon. I floated on my back at the end of the pool and breathed in the rich sensuous aroma of Aunt Zell's forty-year-old bushes. More than magnolias, gardenias are the smell of summer in central North Carolina and their scent unlocks memories and images we never think of when the weather's cool and crisp.

Blurred stars twinkled in the hazy night sky, an occasional plane passed far overhead and lightning bugs drifted lazily through the evening stillness. Drifting with them, unshackled by gravity, I seemed to float not on water but on the thick sweet air itself, half of my senses disoriented, the other half too wholly relaxed to care whether a particular point of light was insect, human or extrater-restrial.

The house is only a few blocks from the center of Dobbs, but our sidewalks roll up at nine on a week night, and there was nothing to break the small town silence except light traffic or the occasional bark of a dog. When I heard the back screen door slam, I assumed it was Aunt Zell or Uncle Ash coming out to

say goodnight, but the man silhouetted against the house lights was too big and
bulky. One of my brothers?

"Deb'rah?" Dwight Bryant moved cautiously down the path and along the
edge of the pool, as if his eyes hadn't yet adjusted to the darkness.

"Watch out you don't fall in," I told him. "Unless you mean to."

I didn't reckon he did because my night vision was good enough to see that
he had on his new sports jacket. As chief of detectives for the Colleton County
Sheriff's Department, Dwight seldom wears a uniform unless he wants to look
particularly official.

He followed my voice and came over to squat down on the coping and dip
a hand in the water.

"Not very cool, is it?"

"Feels good though. Come on in."

"No suit," he said regretfully, "and Mr. Ash is so skinny, I couldn't get into
one of his."

"Oh, you don't need a bathing suit," I teased. "Not dark as it is tonight.
Besides, we're just home folks here."

Dwight snorted. Growing up, he was in and out of our farmhouse so much
that he really could have been one more brother, but my brothers never went
skinny-dipping if I were around. (Correction: not if they knew I was around.
Kid sisters don't always announce their presence.)

"You're working late," I said. "What's up?"

"A young woman over in Black Creek got herself shot dead this morning.
They didn't find her till nearly six this evening."

"Shot? You mean murdered?"

"Looks like it."

"Someone we know?"

"Chastity Barefoot? Everybody called her Chass."

Rang no bells with me.

"She and her husband both grew up in Harnett County. His name's Edward
Barefoot."

"Now that sounds familiar for some reason." I stood up—the lap pool's
only four feet deep—and Dwight reached down his big hand to haul me out
beside him. I came up dripping and wrapped a towel around me as I tried to

think where I'd heard that name recently. "They any kin to the Cotton Grove Barefoots?"

"Not that he said."

I finished drying off and slipped on my flip-flops and an oversized tee- shirt and we walked back to the patio to sit and talk. Aunt Zell came out with a pitcher of iced tea and said she and Uncle Ash were going upstairs to watch the news in bed so if I'd lock up after Dwight left, she'd tell us goodnight now.

I gave her a hug and Dwight did, too, and after she'd gone inside and we were sipping the strong cold tea, I said, "This Edward Barefoot. He do the shooting?"

"Don't see how he could've," said Dwight. "Specially since you're his alibi."

"Come again?"

"He says he spent all morning in your courtroom. Says you let him off with PJC."

"I did?"

Monday morning traffic court is such a cattle call that it's easy for the faces to blur and if Dwight had waited a week to ask me, I might not have remembered. As it was, it took me a minute to sort out which one had been Edward Barefoot,

As a district court judge, I had been presented with minor assaults, drug possession, worthless checks and a dozen other misdemeanor categories; but on the whole, traffic violations had made up the bulk of the day's calendar. Seated on the side benches had been uniformed state troopers and officers from both the town's police department and the county sheriffs department, each prepared to testify why he had ticketed and/or arrested his share of the two hundred and five individuals named on my docket today. Tracy Johnson, the prosecuting ADA, had efficiently whittled at least thirty-five names from that docket and she spent the midmorning break period processing the rest of those who planned to plead guilty without an attorney.

At least 85% were male and younger than thirty. There doesn't seem to be a sexual pattern on who will come up with phony registrations, improper plates or expired inspection stickers, but most sessions have one young lead-footed female and one older female alcoholic who's blown more than the legal point-oh-eight. Yeah, and every week I get at least one middle-aged man who thinks it's his God-given right to keep driving even though his license has been so thoroughly revoked that for the rest of his life it'll barely be legal for him to get behind the steering wheel of a bumper car at the State Fair.

As I poured Dwight a second glass of tea, I remembered seeing Edward Barefoot come up to the defense table. I had wondered whether he was a first-time speeder or someone on the edge of getting his license revoked. His preppie haircut was so fresh that there was a half-inch band of white around the back edges where his hair had kept his neck from tanning, and his neat charcoal gray suit bespoke a young businessman somewhat embarrassed at finding himself in traffic court and eager to make a good impression. His pin-striped shirt and sober tie said, "I'm an upstanding taxpayer and solid citizen of the community," but his edgy good looks would have been more appropriate on one of our tight-jeaned speed jockeys.

Tracy had withdrawn the charge of driving without a valid license, but Barefoot was still left with an 80 in a 65 speed zone.

I nodded to the spit-polished highway patrolman and said, "Tell me about it."

It was the same old same old with a slight variation. Late one evening, about a week earlier, defendant got himself pulled for excessive speed on the interstate that bisects Colleton County. According to the trooper, Mr. Barefoot had been cooperative when asked to step out of the car, but there was an odor of an impairing substance about him and he didn't have his wallet or license.

"Mr. Barefoot stated that his wife was usually their designated driver, so he often left his wallet at home when they went out like that. Just put some cash in his pocket. Mrs. Barefoot was in the vehicle and she did possess a valid license, but she stated that they'd been to a party over in Raleigh and she got into the piña colladas right heavy so they felt like it'd be safer for him to drive."

"Did he blow for you?" I asked.

"Yes, ma'am. He registered a point-oh-five, three points below the legal limit. And there was nothing out of the way about his speech or appearance, other than the speeding. He stated that was because they'd promised the babysitter they'd be home before midnight and they were late. The vehicle was registered in both their names and Mr. Barefoot showed me his license before court took in this morning."

When it was his turn to speak, Barefoot freely acknowledged that he'd been driving 'way too fast, said he was sorry, and requested a PJC, or prayer for judgment continued. In North Carolina, when a defendant pleads guilty to a minor charge, a judge can give him a PJC, which means that he will not have a criminal record for the offense and will not get points against his insurance.

"Any previous violations?" I asked the trooper.

"I believe he has one speeding violation. About three years ago. Sixty-four in a fifty-five zone."

"Only one?" That surprised me because this Edward Barefoot sure looked like a racehorse.

"Just one, your honor," the trooper had said.

"Another week and his only violation would have been neutralized," I told Dwight now as I refilled my glass of iced tea, "so I let him off. Phyllis Raynor was clerking for me this morning and she or Tracy might have a better fix on the time, but I'd say he was out of there by eleven- thirty."

"That late, hmm?"

You'd like for it to be earlier?"

"Well, we think she was killed sometime mid-morning and that would give us someplace to start. Not that we've heard of any trouble between them, but you know how it is—husbands and boyfriends, we always look hard at them first. Barefoot says he got a chicken biscuit at Bojangles on his way out of town, and then drove straight to work. If he got to his job when he says he did, he didn't have enough time to drive home first. That's almost fifty miles. And if he really was in court from nine till eleven-thirty—?"

"Tracy could probably tell you," I said again.

According to Dwight, Chastity Barefoot had dropped her young daughter off at a day care there in Black Creek at nine-thirty that morning and then returned to the little starter home she and her husband had bought the year before in one of the many subdivisions that have sprung up since the new interstate opened and made our cheap land and low taxes attractive to people working around Raleigh. She was a part- time receptionist for a dentist in Black Creek and wasn't due in till noon; her husband worked for one of the big pharmaceuticals in the Research Triangle Park.

When she didn't turn up at work on time, the office manager had first called and then driven out to the house on her lunch hour because "And I quote," said Dwight, "'Whatever else Chass did, she never left you hanging.'"

"Whatever else?" I asked.

"Yeah, she did sort of hint that Miz Barefoot might've had hinges on her heels."

"So there was trouble between the Barefoots."

"Not according to the office manager." Dwight slapped at a mosquito buzzing around his ears. "She says the poor bastard didn't have a clue. Thought Chass hung the moon just for him. Anyhow, Chass's car was there, but the house was locked and no one answered the door, so she left again."

He brushed away another mosquito, drained his tea glass and stood up to go. "I'll speak to Tracy and Phyllis and we'll check every inch of Barefoot's alibi, but I have a feeling we're going to be hunting the boyfriend on this one."

That would have been the end of it as far as I was concerned except that Chastity Barefoot's grandmother was a friend of Aunt Zell's, so Aunt Zell felt she ought to attend the visitation on Wednesday evening. The only trouble was that Uncle Ash had to be out of town and she doesn't like to drive that far alone at night.

"You sure you don't mind?" she asked me that morning.

On a hot Wednesday night, I had planned nothing more exciting than reading briefs in front of the air conditioner in my sitting room.

I had originally moved in with Aunt Zell and Uncle Ash because I couldn't afford a place of my own when I first came back to Colleton County and there was no way I'd have gone back to the farm at that point. I use the self-contained efficiency apartment they fixed for Uncle Ash's mother while she was still alive, with its own separate entrance and relative privacy. We're comfortable together—too comfortable say some of my sisters-in-law who worry that I may never get married—but Uncle Ash has to be away so much, my being there gives everybody peace of mind.

No big deal to drive to the funeral home over in Harnett County, I told her.

It was still daylight, another airless, humid evening and even in a thin cotton dress and barefoot sandals, I had to keep the air conditioner on high most of the way. As we drove, Aunt Zell reminisced about her friend, Retha Minshew, and how sad it was that her little great-granddaughter would probably grow up without any memory of her mother.

"And when Edward remarries, that'll loosen the ties to the Minshews even more," she sighed.

I pricked up my ears. "You knew them? They weren't getting along?"

"No, no. I just mean that he's young and he's got a baby girl that's going to need a mother. Only natural if he took another wife after a while."

"So why did you say 'even more'?" I asked, as I passed a slow-moving pickup truck with three hounds in the back.

"Did I?" She thought about her words. "Maybe it's because the Minshews are so nice and those Barefoots—"

Trust Aunt Zell to know them root and stock.

They say Edward's real steady and hard-working. Always putting in overtime at his office. Works nine or ten hours a day. But the rest of his family—" She hesitated, not wanting to speak badly of anybody. "I think his father spent some time in jail for beating up on his mother.

"Both of them were too drunk to come to the wedding, Retha says. And Retha says his two younger brothers are wild as turkeys, too. Anyhow, I get the impression the Minshews don't do much visiting back and forth with the Barefoots."

Angier is still a small town, but so many people had turned out for the wake that the line stretched across the porch, down the walk and out onto the sidewalk.

Fortunately, the lines usually move fast, and within a half-hour Aunt Zell and I were standing before the open casket. There was no sign that Chastity Minshew Barefoot had died violently. Her fair head lay lightly on the pink satin pillow, her face was smooth and unwrinkled and her pink lips hinted at secret amusement. Her small hands were clasped around a silver picture frame that held a color photograph of a suntanned little girl with curly blond hair.

A large bouquet of gardenias lay on the closed bottom half of the polished casket and the heavy sweet smell was almost overpowering.

Aunt Zell sighed, then turned to the tall gray-haired woman with red-rimmed eyes who stood next to the coffin. "Oh, Retha, honey, I'm just so sorry."

They hugged each other. Aunt Zell introduced me to Chastity's grandmother, who in turn introduced us to her son and daughter-in-law, both of whom seemed shell-shocked by the murder of their daughter.

As did Edward Barefoot, who stood just beyond them. His eyes were glazed and feverish looking. Gone was the crisp young businessman of two days ago. Tonight his face was pinched, his skin was pasty, his hair disheveled. He looked five years older and if they hadn't told me who he was, I wouldn't have recognized him.

He gazed at me blankly as Aunt Zell and I paused to give our condolences. A lot of people don't recognize me without the black robe.

"I'm Judge Knott," I reminded him. "You were in my courtroom day before yesterday. I'm really sorry about your wife."

"Thank you, Judge." His eyes focused on my face and he gave me a firm handshake. "And I want to thank you again for going so easy on me."

"Not at all," I said inanely and was then passed on to his family, a rough-looking couple who seemed uncomfortable in this formal setting, and a self-conscious youth who looked so much like Edward Barefoot that I figured he was the youngest brother. He and his parents just nodded glumly when Aunt Zell and I expressed our sympathy.

As we worked our way back through the crowd, both of us were aware of a different pitch to the usual quiet, funeral home murmur. I spotted a friend out on the porch and several people stopped Aunt Zell for a word. It was nearly half an hour before we got back to my car and both of us had heard the same stories. The middle Barefoot brother had been slipping around with Chastity and he hadn't been seen since she was killed.

"Wonder if Dwight knows?" asked Aunt Zell.

"Yeah, we heard," said Dwight when I called him that evening. "George Barefoot. He's been living at home since he got out of jail and—"

Jail?" I asked.

"Yeah. He ran a stop sign back last November and hit a Toyota. Totaled both cars and nearly killed the other driver. He blew a ten and since he already had one DWI and a string of speeding tickets, Judge Longmire gave him some jail time, too. According to his mother, he hasn't been home since Sunday night. He and the youngest brother are rough carpenters on that new subdivision over off Highway Forty-eight, but the crew chief says he hasn't seen George since quitting time Friday evening. The two brothers claim not to know where he is either."

"Are they lying?"

I could almost hear Dwight's shrug over the phone. "Who knows?"

"You put out an APB on his vehicle?"

"He doesn't have one. Longmire pulled his license. Wouldn't even give him driving privileges during work hours. That's why he's been living at home. So he could ride to work with his brother Paul."

"The husband's alibi hold up?"

"Solid as a tent pole. It's a forty-mile roundtrip to his house. Tracy says he answered the calendar call around nine-thirty—that's when his wife was dropping their kid off at the day care—and you entered his " between eleven-fifteen and eleven-thirty. Lucky for him, he kept his Bojangles receipt. It's the one out on the bypass, and the time on it says twelve-oh-five. It's another forty minutes to his work, and they say he was there before one o'clock and didn't leave till after five, so it looks like he's clear."

More than anybody could say for his brother George.

Poor Edward Barefoot. From what I now knew about that bunch of Barefoots, he was the only motivated member of his family. The only one to finish high school, he'd even earned an associate degree at the community college. Here was somebody who could be the poster child for bootstrapping, a man who'd worked hard and played by the rules, and what happens? Bad enough to lose the wife you adore, but then to find out she's been cheating with your sorry brother who probably shot her and took off?

Well, it wasn't for me to condemn Chass Barefoot's taste in men. I've danced with the devil enough times myself to know the attraction of no-'count charmers.

Aunt Zell went to the funeral the next day and described it for Uncle Ash and me at supper.

"That boy looked like he was strung out on the rack. And his precious little baby! Her hair's blond like her mama's, but she's been out in her wading pool so much this summer, Retha said, that she's brown as a pecan." She put a hot and fluffy biscuit on my plate. "It just broke my heart to see the way she kept her arms wrapped around her daddy's neck as if she knew her mama was gone forever. But she's only two, way too young to understand something like that."

From my experience with children who come to family court having suffered enormous loss and trauma, I knew that a two-year-old was indeed too young to understand or remember, yet something about Aunt Zell's description of the little girl kept troubling me.

For her sake, I hoped that George Barefoot would be arrested and quickly brought to trial so that her family could find closure and healing.

Unfortunately, it didn't happen quite that way because two days later, George Barefoot's body was found when some county workers were cleaning up an illegal trash dump on one of the back roads just north of Dobbs. He was lying on an old sofa someone had thrown into the underbrush, and the high back had concealed him from the road.

The handgun he'd stuck in his mouth had landed on some dirt and leaves beside the sofa. It was the same gun that had killed Chastity Barefoot, a gun she'd bought to protect herself from intruders. There was a note in his pocket addressed to his brother:

E — God, I'm so sorry about
Chass. I never meant to hurt you.
You know how much you mean
to me.
Love always,
George

A rainy night and several hot humid days had mildewed the note and blurred the time of death, but the M.E. thought he could have shot himself either the day Chastity Barefoot was killed or no later than the day after.

That road's miles from his mother's house," I told Dwight. "Wonder why he picked it? And how did he get there?"

Dwight shrugged. "It's just a few hundred feet from where Highway 70 crosses the bypass. Maybe he was hitchhiking out of the county and that's where his ride put him out. Maybe he got to feeling remorse and knew he couldn't run forever. Who knows?"

I was in Dwight's office that noonday, waiting for him to finish reading over the file so that he could send it on to our District Attorney, official notification that the two deaths could be closed out. A copy of the suicide note lay on his desk and I'm as curious as any cat.

"Can I see that?"

"Sure."

The original was locked up of course, but this was such a clear photocopy that I could see every spot of mildew and the ragged edge of where Barefoot must have torn the page from a notepad.

"Was there a notepad on his body?" I asked idly.

"No, and no pencil either," said Dwight. "He must have written it before leaving wherever he was holed up."

I made a doubtful noise and he looked at me in exasperation. "Don't go trying to make a mystery out of this, Deb'rah. He was bonking his sister-in-law, things got messy, so he shot her and then he shot himself. Nobody else has a motive, nobody else could've done it."

"The husband had motive."

"The husband was in your court at the time, remember?" He stuck the suicide note back in the file and stood up. "Let's go eat."

"Bonking?" I asked as we walked across the street to the Soup 'n' Sandwich Shop.

He gave a rueful smile. "Cal's starting to pick up language. I promised Jonna I'd clean up my vocabulary."

Jonna is Dwight's ex-wife and a real priss-pot.

"You don't talk dirty," I protested, but he wouldn't argue the point. When our waitress brought us our barbecue sandwiches, I noticed that her ring finger was conspicuously bare. Instead of a gaudy engagement ring, there was now only a thin circle of white skin.

"Don't tell me you and Conrad have broken up again?" I said.

Angry sparks flashed from her big blue eyes. "Good riddance to bad rubbish."

Dwight grinned at me when she was gone. "Want to bet how long before she's wearing his ring again?"

I shook my head. It would be a sucker bet.

Instead, I found myself looking at Dwight's hands as he bit into his sandwich. He had given up wearing a wedding band as soon as Jonna walked out on him, so his fingers were evenly tanned by the summer sun. Despite all the paperwork in his job, he still got out of the office a few hours every day. I reached across and pulled on the expansion band of his watch.

"What-?"

"Just checking," I said. "Your wrist is white."

"Of course it is. I always wear my watch. Aren't you going to eat your sandwich?"

My appetite was fading, so I cut it in two and gave him half.

"Hurry up and eat," I said. "I want to see that suicide note again before I have to go back to court."

Grumbling, he wolfed down his lunch; and even though his legs are much longer than mine, he had to stretch them out to keep up as I hurried back to his office.

"What?" he asked, when I was studying the note again.

"I think you ought to let the SBI's handwriting experts take a closer look at this."

"Why?"

Well, look at it," I said, pointing to the word *about* which jutted into the margin.

"And see that little mark after *sorry*? Couldn't that be a comma? What if the original version was just *'I'm sorry, Chass?'* What if somebody also added that capital E to make you think it was a note to Edward when it was probably a love letter to Chastity?"

"Huh?" Dwight took the paper from my hand and looked at it closer.

We've known each other so long he can almost read my mind at times.

"But Edward Barefoot was in court when his wife was shot. He couldn't be two places at one time."

"Yes, he could," I said and told him how.

I cut court short that afternoon so that I'd be there when they brought Edward Barefoot in for questioning.

He denied everything and called for an attorney.

"I was in traffic court," he told Dwight when his attorney was there and questioning resumed. "Ask the judge here." He turned to me with a hopeful look. "You let me off with a prayer for judgment". You said so yourself at the funeral home."

"I was mistaken," I said gently. "It was your brother George that I let off. You three brothers look so much alike that when I saw you at the funeral home, I had no reason not to think you were the same man who'd been in court. I didn't immediately recognize you, but I thought that was because you were in shock. You're not in shock right now, though. This is your natural color."

Puzzled, his attorney said, "I beg your pardon?"

"He puts in ten or twelve hours a day at an office, so he isn't tan. The man who stood before my bench had just had a fresh haircut and he was so tanned that it left a ring of white around the hairline. When's the last time you had a haircut, Mr. Barefoot?"

He touched his hair. Clearly, it was normally short and neat. Just as clearly, he hadn't visited a barber in three or four weeks. "I've— Everything's been so—"

"Don't answer that," said his attorney.

I thought about his little daughter's nut-brown arms clasped tightly around his pale neck and I wasn't happy about where this would end for her.

"When the trooper stopped your wife's car for speeding, your brother knew he'd be facing more jail time if he gave his right name. So he gave your name instead. He could rattle off your address and birthdate glibly enough to satisfy the trooper. Then all he had to do was show up in court with your driver's license and your clean record and act respectable and contrite. Did you know he was out with Chastity that night?"

Like a stuck needle, the attorney said, "Don't answer that."

"The time and date would be on any speeding ticket he showed you," said Dwight. "Along with the license number and make of the car."

"She said she was at her friend's in Raleigh and that his girlfriend had dumped him and he was hitching a ride home," Edward burst out over the protest of his attorney. "Like I was stupid enough to believe that after everything else!"

"So you made George get a haircut, lent him a suit and tie, dropped him at the courthouse, with your driver's license, and then went back to your house and killed Chastity. After court, you met George here in Dobbs, killed him and dumped his body on the way out of town."

"We'll find people who were in the courtroom last Monday morning and can testify about his appearance," said Dwight. "We'll find the barber. We may even find your fingerprints on the note."

Edward Barefoot seemed to shrink down into the chair.

"You don't have to respond to any of these accusations," said his attorney. "They're just guessing."

Guessing?

Maybe.

Half of life is guesswork.

The little Barefoot girl might be only two years old, but I'm guessing that she'll never be allowed to forget that her daddy killed her mama. Especially when gardenias are in bloom.

— *Shoveling Smoke: Selected Mystery Stories*, Crippen & Landru, 1997

Chronologically, this story occurs between Storm Track *and* Uncommon Clay.

THE THIRD ELEMENT

"It's all Douglas Woodall's fault," Miss Eula declared as she waved away the plate of homemade cookies Aunt Zell was offering for dessert. "How could he be so mean as to prosecute Kyle?"

Aunt Zell passed the plate to me. "Well, Kyle did sort of shoot that Wentworth boy," she said, trying to be fair.

(Which was putting it as tactfully as possible since Miss Eula's grandson had done a lot more than "sort of" shoot Hux Wentworth. Kyle Benson had actually emptied all nine rounds of a 9mm automatic into Hux's back while Hux lay wounded on the floor.)

"But it was self-defense," Miss Eula insisted, as Kyle himself had insisted ever since it happened last fall. "Are you supposed to let yourself be beaten to a bloody pulp before you can defend yourself? You're a judge, Deborah. Is that really what the law says?"

"Not exactly," I answered, speaking around one of Aunt Zell's lemon crisps. As a district court judge who will never hear a murder case of any sort, I could take the academic view. "You can use force to defend yourself, but the third element of self-defense, the one that says you can use deadly force, means that you have to be afraid for your life. Doug Woodall's saying that once Wentworth was down and wounded, Kyle and Brinley could have escaped without killing him. Their lives were no longer in danger and Kyle shouldn't have kept shooting."

Actually, considering how many bullet holes they found in Hux Wentworth's back and considering the previous history between those two, Miss Eula's grandson was lucky that our DA hadn't asked the grand jury to hand down an indictment for second-degree murder rather than voluntary manslaughter.

And despite Miss Eula's huffing, Doug had considerately waited till after Kyle graduated from Carolina this past June instead of pushing to calendar the case months earlier.

Now it was July and the whole Benson clan was camped out in the courtroom while the prosecution and defense went through the tedious and time-consuming process of picking a jury.

Miss Eula is their matriarch and she's also the oldest living member of Bethel Baptist Church out in the country where Mother and Aunt Zell often visited when they were growing up. Mindful of her advanced age and the thirty-minute drive to and from Dobbs, Aunt Zell had invited Miss Eula to come for lunch every day and then to lie down for a little rest afterwards before going back over to the courtroom.

Miss Eula's will is strong, but her body's frail so she'd made only token demurrals before accepting, although she still blamed Doug Woodall for all the inconvenience. "See if any of us ever contribute to his campaign again," she said darkly.

Poor Doug. He was between a rock and a hard place on this one.

Elections are usually a cake walk for our District Attorney, but this time around, he has serious opposition and he's been accused of going easy on people of substance (which the Bensons are) and of not going after a killer as vigorously when the victim is of a lesser social class (which Hux Wentworth certainly was).

While it's true that Doug doesn't exactly bust his budget when one migrant worker kills another over a bottle of Richard's Wild Irish Rose and then flees the state, he does care when residents get themselves killed, even when that resident is somebody as sorry and no good as Hux Wentworth.

The Wentworths were always a violent family, root and stock. Hux's brother is sitting in State Prison right now for murder and Hux himself had served a short term up in Raleigh for armed robbery. But he was big and handsome and could turn on a rough sort of charm when he chose to.

Having danced with the devil a time or three myself, I can understand how a nice girl like Brinley Davis could let herself be blindsided by a bad boy "misunderstood" by everyone else. Unfortunately, she had to learn by experience that if you're gonna pick up trash, you're gonna get your hands dirty before you can turn it loose.

Hux Wentworth wasn't a piece of mud to be scraped off the heel of a summer sandal. He was bubblegum, twice as messy, twice as sticky, and when Brinley tried to tell him that she was interested in someone else–Kyle Benson, in this case–Hux's first reaction was to threaten to beat the living-you-know-what out of Kyle. Since Kyle is built like a wiry tennis player and Hux had the bulk of a linebacker, it was lucky that Kyle was back in Chapel Hill by the time Brinley told him this or it might be Hux standing trial for Kyle's death instead of the other way around.

Actually, if you could believe Brinley and Kyle, that's nearly the way it was.

I had heard their story from Miss Eula. I'd heard it from Sheriff's Deputy Dwight Bryant, who was first detective on the scene. I'd also heard it from just about anybody else who could get me to stand still long enough to speculate about Kyle's guilt or innocence with them, including Portland Brewer, my best friend and Kyle's attorney. At this point, everybody in Colleton County had heard it. The main facts were not in dispute:

a) Brinley Davis had told Hux Wentworth she didn't want to see him again.

b) Hux Wentworth said he'd kill Kyle Benson and Brinley, too, if she tried to go out with Kyle.

c) At fall break, Brinley stayed home while her parents drove out to the mountains to see the leaves. (Portland's eyebrows had arched slyly when she told me, "Brinley said she'd seen leaves before.") Her parents probably hadn't even cleared the Dobbs town limits before Brinley called Kyle and told him she was nervous about being all alone in that big house. (So okay, little Brinley's not a pure-as-the-driven-snow-princess. Who is, these days?)

d) Brinley and Kyle were snuggled on a couch in the den watching a video when Hux crashed through the french doors.

Literally. Without even trying the knob.

Unfortunately for him, French doors are built more sturdily than he realized and while he stood there, momentarily dazed and bleeding from a dozen superficial cuts, Brinley and Kyle took off like a pair of terrified rabbits.

According to Dwight, Hux left a trail of blood and glass as he tracked the two through the house, up the broad staircase, along the hall, to the master bedroom where Brinley remembered that her daddy kept a loaded automatic pistol in the night stand. She hastily dug it out of the drawer, thrust it into Kyle's hands, then dragged him into her parents' bathroom, locking the door behind them.

That door was even stronger than the french doors, but Hux kicked it open with a mighty roar.

At this point, depending on who's telling it, the tale splits. According to Brinley and Kyle, they were in fear of their lives.

"Shoot, Kyle, shoot!" Brinley screamed, whereupon Kyle Benson emptied the gun, all nine slugs, into Hux Wentworth.

Seven of those slugs hit him in the back—as he was trying to flee, said our District Attorney—and it was on the basis of those seven extra shots, two of them fired while Hux was lying face-down on the bathroom tiles that Kyle had been charged with voluntary manslaughter.

Now it was going to be up to twelve citizens of Colleton County to decide.

"So how did your jury shape up?" I asked Portland when we met for an early supper two evenings later at a local steak and ale place that overlooks the river. With her husband out of town and my guy a hundred miles away, we were both at loose ends.

"Who knows?" she shrugged wearily. Jury selection had finished that morning and opening arguments had begun that afternoon with nothing more than a lunch break.

Ned O'Donnell, the superior court judge who was hearing this case, runs a tight ship. He is very solicitous of jurors and keeps things moving so they aren't inconvenienced a minute longer than necessary.

Voir dire (questioning prospective jurors) is always tiring and Portland looked drained as she ticked the results off on her fingers.

"We wound up with five middle-aged white women—a schoolteacher, beautician, social worker, file clerk and daycare worker, and one elderly black woman who used to keep house for the governor's great aunt. Judge O'Donnell offered to let her off because of her age, but she said she wanted to do her civic duty. Two black men—an orderly from the hospital and a retired black postal worker, and four white men—two farmers, a sheet rocker, and a driver for Ferncliff Sausage who has tattoos from his wrists to his shoulders."

"Like Hux Wentworth?" I asked, drizzling a little olive oil over my salad of mixed summer greens.

"Exactly like," Portland nodded. "But he didn't give me any grounds to challenge for cause and I didn't want to use up my last peremptory challenge in case the next person was worse."

"Maybe he'll scare some of the women enough to let them sympathize with Kyle," I said, offering what comfort I could.

She laughed and took a sip of her beer. "Want to split a steak?"

"Sure," I said. We've been splitting food since grade school.

"Another beer for y'all?" asked the waitress even though our glasses were still more than half full. We shook our heads and she went off with our order.

We spoke of this and that, but Portland kept circling back to Doug Woodall's eloquent opening argument.

"Oh, Doug," I said dismissively. "He has to put on a strong case, but you're not really worried, are you?"

"I don't know, Deborah, and that's a fact. We've got a great expert witness, an ME who can explain those shots in the back—"

"He can?"

"She."

"Uh-oh. Mistake right there," I warned. "A woman disputing the word of a male expert in front of a Colleton County jury?"

"Don't try to teach your grandma how to suck eggs," Portland said smugly. "The state's ME is a woman, too."

She held up her hand to illustrate Wentworth's torso and her expert witness's interpretation of the angles of penetration.

"The first slug hit him in the hand. The next one in the shoulder. The force of the first two bullets spun him around—" She twisted her hand and slowly bent it back. "—so that the next seven caught him across the back as he was going down. Kyle didn't shoot him on the floor, it's just that the angle changed as Hux was falling away from them."

"Okay," I conceded, playing devil's advocate, "but Kyle grew up with guns. He knows what one bullet can do. How you going to explain away nine of them?"

"That's what Doug argued."

"And your response?"

"Yes, ladies and gentlemen of the jury, Kyle Benson did indeed grow up with rifles, shotguns and an old-fashioned revolver, but—" She paused dramatically. "—he'd never fired an automatic before."

Our steak and two plates arrived and I divided the filet right down the middle while Portland did the same with our single baked potato. We'd forgone the Texas toast and made the waitress take the sour cream and butter back to the kitchen so that neither of us would yield to temptation in the middle of swimsuit season. The steak was grilled just the way we like it—almost crusty black on the outside, bright red on the inside—and that first bite awakened the carnivore that slumbers deep in my taste buds. Much as I adore fruits and vegetables, every once in a while I take a truly sensuous pleasure in red meat.

"Mmmm!" Portland murmured happily, echoing my own enjoyment.

"You ever fire an automatic?" she asked, unable to keep her mind off the case.

I nodded. From my own days as a trial lawyer, I remembered this obsession to keep going over and over the facts.

"Well, then, you know that once you pull on that trigger, it'll keep firing till you release the pressure. The gun's empty almost as soon as you start. And don't forget our ear witnesses."

"Ah, yes, the McCormacks."

I've met them and wasn't particularly taken with either. They're from Connecticut. He's upper management in one of the high-tech corporations over in the Research Triangle. Very fond of the sound of his own voice. She's a listener. Reminds me a little of the way Nancy Reagan used to listen adoringly whenever Ronnie spoke.

The McCormacks live next door to the Davises if you can call houses set squarely in the middle of acre lots and surrounded by lots of mature trees and shrubbery "next door." The McCormacks planned to host a large brunch on their patio the next morning so they were outside, making last minute preparations, wiping down the patio furniture, setting up the extra tables on the edge of the back lawn.

When Kyle and Brinley fled her house that night, they had headed straight for the bright lights of the McCormacks' patio.

"Doug's opening statement kept stressing that there was no way Kyle didn't know that those first two shots hit Hux and put him on the floor," Portland told me. "He's going to try to get McCormack to say that Kyle and Brinley were exaggerating their fear, but he can't get around the fact that McCormack heard all the shots and that he's positive there wasn't a break between them."

She gave me an ironic smile. "Unlike Fred Bissell."

I smiled, too, remembering a client my cousin John Claude had defended last year. Mr. Bissell claimed he shot both his wife and the man she was in bed with in the heat of the moment. Unfortunately, three neighbors swore there was a long pause between the first two shots and the last two—one bullet for the wife, three for her lover. He's currently serving a nineteen-to-thirty—not what Portland had in mind for young Kyle Benson.

"What about Mrs. McCormack?" I asked.

Portland shrugged. "She just echoes what her husband says. And you know how Judge O'Donnell feels about superfluous witnesses who don't bring anything new to the table."

Indeed. Doesn't matter if it's prosecution or defense, Ned never hesitates to apologize to the jury for having their time wasted by either side. Doesn't take much to have a jury turn against you.

"What's really worrying me is the way Doug's harping on that old Little League accident," said Portland. "Trying to make it sound as if Kyle and Hux had such a blood feud going that Kyle took this opportunity to deliberately get rid of a lifelong enemy. Hell! They were kids. Kyle barely remembers it."

"He might not," I said reluctantly, "but from what I hear, Hux Wentworth did."

My nephew Reese had been playing the night it happened and half my family were there to cheer him on. It was his and Hux's last year of Little League and Kyle's first. Kyle was small but he had an arm and the beginning of a good fast ball. His team was so far behind the coach decided to put him in for a little seasoning and Kyle was told to go out and pitch as hard as he could.

First up was Hux Wentworth, who had a tendency to crowd the plate. Kyle's first pitch was over Hux's head. His second was dead on the money. It would have been a called strike except that it slammed into Hux's hand gripping the bat directly over the inside corner of the plate. Broke the index and middle fingers of his right hand.

Outraged, Hux had stormed the pitcher's mound. It took both coaches, the umpire and my nephew Reese to stop him and in the melee, the fingers were so badly hurt that by the time Hux's mother figured her home remedies weren't working and carried him to a doctor, there was irreparable nerve damage.

According to Reese, Hux forever after blamed Kyle for ruining his potential baseball career. The hand still functioned well enough for most things, but Hux could no longer control his slider, his "money pitch," as he called it.

"Did he really have that much potential?" I'd asked Reese back when the shooting occurred last fall and that old Little League story had resurfaced.

"Nah," Reese had said scornfully. "His slider that he keeps bitching about? It was an okay pitch, but it was all he had and I guess it got to seem like more the older we got. It was like, here was Kyle with his rich family, that new car they gave him, finishing college and all, and that pissed Hux big time 'cause he won't going nowhere. Didn't even finish high school. Like he'd've had all that stuff, too, if Kyle didn't break his fingers? Yeah. Right."

This from my nephew who barely scraped through high school himself, drives a pickup and seems perfectly content to go on working off my brother's electrician's license for the rest of his life.

"And then when Brinley Davis dumped him, I heard Hux was like, 'He took my slider and now he's taking my girl? I'll cut off his effing balls.' And I guess he would've if Kyle didn't shoot him. They say he had a knife with him that night."

"No knife," Portland said regretfully, when I repeated Reese's words. "And Doug's subpoenaed Brinley as a hostile witness. Going to try to make her admit that she'd told Kyle that Hux was bearing a grudge and that Kyle was taking it seriously."

"Hard to prove a negative," I said, quoting one of our law professors at Carolina.

Even though we're practically the same age, Portland kept her life on track back then and graduated from law school three years ahead of me. Despite the time difference, we'd taken courses from many of the same professors.

"Dr. Gaustaad." She pinched her nose to imitate his distinctive pedantic twang. "'Never ask a question you don't know the answer to.'"

I pinched my own nose and chanted, "'Always interview your witnesses at least three times.'"

We were laughing so hard I almost choked on my last swallow of steak. The waitress came by and tried to offer us dessert, but we were good and ordered cups of plain black coffee.

"Did you?" I asked.

"Did I what?" Portland asked, looking wistful as the dessert cart, with its generous portions of bourbon-pecan pie and double chocolate brownies, rolled away from us.

"Interview all your witnesses at least three times?"

"Sure."

"Really?"

"Well, all but Bill McCormack," she admitted. "He's so full of himself. I interviewed him twice and read the transcript of the deposition Doug Woodall's staff took and he didn't change a word of his story."

"All the same," I said, "if Doug's going to try to show Kyle's state of mind with McCormack's testimony..."

With her very short, very curly black hair, Portland always reminds me of Julia Lee's poodle. At the moment, she was looking like a rather worried poodle.

Here in July, it wasn't quite dark outside at this hour, but it would have been pitch black in October.

"You interviewed him in the daylight, right?" I said.

She nodded.

"Why don't you go back and interview him now, when it's dark? Get him to take you out on the patio, turn on the lights and recreate the scene. Maybe it'll spark just that one detail that'll make a difference."

"On the other hand," Portland said dubiously, "it might spark a detail I don't want to hear."

"Better to hear it tonight than on the witness stand next week," I told her.

Reluctantly, she reached for her cell phone.

"Come with me?"

The McCormack home was just as I'd expected from meeting the owners: pretentiously tasteful fieldstone, modern without being modernistic, landscaped for ostentatious privacy.

"I understand your reasoning," said Bill McCormack after Portland reintroduced us all around, "but I've already told you and the D.A. both what happened that night and walking through it again isn't going to change anything."

Nevertheless, he led us through the house, into the "great" room, and out a set of sliding glass doors onto a broad flagstone patio. Concealed floodlights washed the area in brilliant light.

While Portland went over the events of that October evening once more with McCormack, I engaged his wife in conversation. She seemed a bit surprised that I wanted to talk to her when her husband was holding forth, but I was curious about an exotic-looking stand of daylilies beside the patio and it turned out that they were hybrids she had bred herself.

"A hobby of mine," she said shyly. "I'm trying to breed a pure red with the stamina of those old orange ditch lilies but with a longer bloom time."

She flipped another switch to illumine a border of more lilies at the far edge of the closely clipped grass. "I have sixteen different varieties here. They start blooming in May and go till frost."

"Really?" As a new homeowner still fumbling along with no clear idea of how I wanted my yard to look, I was intrigued by an ever blooming border that wouldn't take much care.

"Yes, I was so worried when Brinley and her friend came running through it last fall. It was the first year my Alyson Ripley lily had bloomed and I was afraid they'd trample it to pieces."

"The Davis house is over there?" For some reason, I'd thought it was on the opposite side.

"Beyond the crepe myrtles," said Mrs. McCormack with a nod. "They always lose their leaves early and that's how Brinley saw our lights so easily." She shook her head. "Such a terrible experience. They were so scared they didn't look where they were going. Right through my lilies. And the way they kept looking back over their shoulders, I thought I was going to see a pack of dogs at their heels and my border would be wrecked for sure."

"That's my Frances," McCormack said genially as he and Portland came up behind us. "More worried about a few flowers than a man getting shot next door."

He gestured toward the trees. "But this is the way they came all right. First we heard the shots all bunched together, and then while we were trying to decide if we'd really heard shots, they came running through here, across her flower bed and up to where we were standing on the patio. The girl was screaming blue murder and he was yelling, 'Call 911.' You don't have to worry about my story, Ms. Brewer," he said magisterially. "I'm quite sure they weren't acting."

"See?" said Portland when we were back in her car and driving away. "What did I tell you? Daylight, moonlight, his story doesn't change."

I couldn't believe what I was hearing. "You're not still going to call him as your witness, are you?"

"I don't have to. Doug'll do it."

"But didn't you hear what Mrs. McCormack said?" I demanded.

"About her flower bed getting trampled?"

"What are the three essential elements of justifiable homicide?" I asked, pinching my nose la Professor Gaustaad.

She stuck out her tongue but decided to humor me. "First, that the defendant must be free from fault, must not have said or done anything for the purpose of provoking the victim."

"Was Kyle at fault? Did he provoke? No," I said, answering my own rhetorical questions. "He was an invited guest in the Davis home, minding his own business when Hux Wentworth burst through the door. The second element?"

"There must be no convenient mode of escape by retreat or by declining combat," Portland parroted as she put on her turn signal to make a left back to the steakhouse and my own car. "And he did try to retreat but Hux followed and broke through a second locked door."

"And the third element, if you please, Ms. Brewer?"

"There must be a present impending peril, either real or apparent, so as to create in the defendant a reasonable belief of existing necessity. Well, that's exactly what Kyle believed, but how do we prove it?" Portland said with exasperation. "How's Mrs. McCormack's lily bed going to convince a jury he really truly believed it?"

"Okay, look," I told her, spelling it out. "Hux Wentworth is built like Man Mountain, right? He crashes through a glass door, like it was paper. He's bleeding all over, yet he barely notices his cuts. He chases them through the house and crashes through the bathroom door without even breaking a sweat. Kyle pulls the trigger on an unfamiliar gun and as soon as Hux goes down, he and Brinley are out of there. You heard McCormack. They were still trying to figure out what the shots were when those two kids ran into his yard. And they were looking back over their shoulders. Why were they looking back, Por?"

"My God," she exclaimed as she pulled into the steakhouse parking lot and stopped beside my car. "Did they really think Hux could still be chasing them after all that?"

"Why not?" I said. "He'd come through glass, he'd come through solid oak– In their state of panic, why wouldn't they think he could come through bullets?"

A week later, I adjourned my own court early so I could hear Portland's closing argument.

"In their state of panic," Portland said, "why wouldn't they think he could come through bullets, too? You have heard Mrs. McCormick state that when they first stumbled into her yard, only moments after the sound of gunshots died away, they kept glancing back over their shoulders. Why? Would you look back if you knew your attacker was lying dead? No, ladies and gentlemen of the jury. They looked back because they were afraid that Hux Wentworth was still coming after them and they were terrified that he would catch them."

Doug Woodall made a game attempt to persuade the jury that Kyle and Brinley were play-acting, but it didn't work. They were only out long enough to pick a foreman before returning with a not guilty verdict. Ten minutes max.

Ned O'Donnell thanked the jury and then thanked both sides for an expeditious trial. "Not a single superfluous witness," he said approvingly.

Smugly I waited for Portland to finish hugging Kyle and to come thank me, but as soon as we were alone, she said, "I'm writing Professor Gaustaad to thank him for advising at least three interviews."

"Gaustaad?" I was indignant. "Hey, I was the one that made you go back a third time."

"I know," she grinned. "I'm going to thank him for hammering it into your head."

— *A Confederacy of Crime,* Signet, 2000

As soon as I saw a newspaper picture of a modern day pilgrim lugging a wooden cross up and down the eastern seaboard, I knew such a man was going to have to show up in Deborah Knott's courtroom. (Alert readers will spot Carolyn Hart's Annie Darling, who just happens to be a friend of Deborah's.)

MIXED BLESSINGS

The first time I saw it was two years ago. I was driving back from Broward's Rock, an upscale resort island down near the South Carolina-Georgia border. Not a place I could normally afford to vacation in, but my friend Annie owns a bookstore there and had invited me for a long weekend. As the daughter of an ex-bootlegger and someone who grew up sweating through my share of the farmwork, I'm always interested in seeing how the other half live and play.

Anyhow, I had left the island and was heading west on a little two-lane road. Fortunately, the sun had already set, but there was still a blazing gold- and-red afterglow in the western sky. A few miles before I reached 1-95, a reddish light appeared on the right shoulder up ahead. It was as if a ragged patch of glowing sky had dropped onto the roadside and was bobbing along eastward. The car ahead of me slowed to a crawl and I tapped my brakes, too, to warn the car behind.

To my bemusement, it was a full-size plastic cross, illuminated from within so that it gleamed bright red in the twilight. In the brief moment it took me to drive past, I only had time to note that it rode on the back of a sturdily built man with dark hair and ragged beard and a determined look on his face.

A large lighted plastic cross was not the oddest sight I'd ever seen along southern roads—after all, this is the Bible Belt—but it tickled me to picture him lugging it onto the ferry to Broward's Rock. The tiny town at the ferry landing is open to anyone but what about the gated communities that take up most of the island? Would the guards at those gatehouses turn him back or look the other way as he passed? And if he made it through, what would all those wealthy vacationing golfers from up north or the midwest make of him?

I made a mental note to call Annie when I got home and ask, but like so many of my mental notes, it faded before I reached the North Carolina line where Pancho's South of the Border, the ultimate in tacky rest stops, gave me a whole new set of absurdities to contemplate.

The next rime I saw that cross was in the last place I could have imagined: my own church, the First Baptist Church of Dobbs.

Our minister, the Reverend Carlyle Yelvington is a thoughtful, dignified intellectual, as befits the pastor of the oldest and wealthiest Baptist church in Colleton County. He entreats his congregation to lead a moral life by gentle appeals to logic and ethics. Charismatic techniques horrify him and he would never get down and mud-wrestle someone into salvation, but he's smart enough to know that a good rousing fire-and-brimstone sermon can act like a bracing spring tonic for the Baptist soul. Accordingly, he has a carefully screened roster of more dynamic preachers whom he invites to come and witness to us five or six times a year when he has to be away.

Unfortunately, the more dynamic preacher he'd invited this Sunday was himself called away at the last minute, and instead of consulting with Mr. Yelvington's secretary, he took it upon himself to send a substitute of his own choosing, which is how we wound up with Brother Reuben in the pulpit shouting out a message of damnation and redemption, "Yea, even to those amongst you to whom much has been given without you giving back to the Lord who's blessed you with so many worldly goods, who's set you on such a high horse that you think you got in the saddle all by yourself."

In ringing tones, Brother Reuben explained how, only last week, a man of God had appeared in the doorway of his poor little mission down in Fayette-ville, laboring under a heavy burden, "a burden put on him by the Lord Jesus Christ himself, a burden to go out into the highways and byways and preach the word of God. Well, my friends, that's what he's done all week down there in Fayetteville and when I got the call Thursday night to come here this morning, I knew that the Lord had laid a blessing on you and that He wanted Brother Buck to come on up here to Dobbs, to bring his burden into this fine and stately house of worship and preach His word right here."

With that, he turned to the double doors that led back to classrooms and robing room and church offices and shouted, "Brother Buck, in the name of our Lord Jesus Christ, come forth!"

The doors swung open and there was that same bright red cross that I'd first seen in South Carolina, riding on the shoulders of the same dark-bearded man. I now saw that he was older than my brief impression, probably late forties or early fifties. He wore a blue T-shirt imprinted with the words, "I am a soldier of the Cross," and his face and muscular arms were deeply tanned. I also saw that cross was ten feet tall and constructed of bright red Plexiglass, crimson as the blood of Christ. Two little hard-rubber wheels, the kind you see on push mowers, were mounted on an axle through the base of the cross to make it easier to carry, but the thing still must have weighed a ton. When Brother Buck mounted the dais and stood beside Brother Reuben, it towered another four feet above their heads.

Wilma Carter, Mr. Yelvington's elderly secretary, sat in appalled silence in the pew ahead of mine, but my friend Portland Brewer was cracking up beside me.

"Friends," said Brother Reuben, "this is Brother Buck Collins and he's got a message you should open your hearts and hear. Tell 'em, Brother Buck!"

Buck Collins' testimony began with a certain predictability: the dissipated youth, the drugs, the gambling, the drunken nights of wenching and whoring.

Okay, every word might have been true, but over the years I've noticed that reformed sinners tend to—well, not lie exactly, but more like "enhance" the darkness of their sinfulness in order to dramatize the extent of their reformation and redemption.

Anyhow, five years ago, in the depth of his degradation, his sister persuaded him to go to church with her one Sunday morning. The preacher seemed to speak directly to his heart.

"And I went out of that house with my soul on fire, tormented by the flames of hell. That very same night, friends, our Savior appeared to me in a dream, saying 'Go out into the highways and hedges, and compel them to come in, that my house may be filled.' Well, friends, two days later, I set out on my journey with nothing but a back pack and my new faith in the Lord, who promised to provide my daily needs. Even the poorest man is rich when the Lord looks after him."

However, he'd no sooner set out, than he met an evangelist carrying a small cross of two poles lashed together. "As soon as I saw it, I knew immediately that Jesus wanted me to bear His cross, too, so I went back home and got this one built."

("A classic case of penance envy," Portland whispered in my ear.)

He had been on the road ever since, traveling from church to church, mission to mission, spreading the word of redemption and salvation to all he met along the highways and back roads.

"Amen, Jesus!" said Brother Reuben when the testimony ended. "And now I'm gonna ask the choir to lead us in singing "The Old Rugged Cross.""

The choir, which had planned a joyous Purcell anthem, had to scramble for their hymnals and that lugubrious dirge.

Two mornings later, I saw the cross yet again. It was leaning sideways on its base and crosspiece in the hallway outside Major Dwight Bryant's door. Dwight and I have known each other since I was in diapers and he was a lanky kid in and out of our house like one of my eleven older brothers. Since I'm a district court judge now and he's second in command under Sheriff Bowman "Bo" Poole with offices here in the Colleton County Courthouse, we still see each other almost every day; and I often take my lunchbag down to his office while he eats a sandwich at his desk.

Today's was an enormous BLT made with tomatoes from my daddy's garden that I'd brought him the day before. I love BLT's, too, but I'm not six- three, which is why I was eating peach yogurt.

"Don't tell me Brother Buck's in jail here," I said, settling into the chair across from him.

"Change the subject," he told me.

"Why?" I asked indignantly. And then it dawned on me.

"Don't you read your calendar?" he teased.

Well, I do, of course—mostly to see if any of my friends or neighbors are going to be standing in front of me, which happens more often than I'd really like. But my eyes had slid right over the name of Buck Collins, who would be the subject of a probable cause hearing this afternoon. So quite properly, Dwight and I couldn't talk about it, even though I was dying of curiosity.

When his name was called, Buck Collins walked down from the jury box where the jailer had seated all his prisoners. Like the rest of them, Collins was dressed in an orange polyester jump suit. He took his place behind the defendants' table and I asked if he were represented by an attorney.

"No, ma'am," he answered softy.

I explained his right to one should he so desire and how the state would pay the costs if he couldn't afford it. When he shook his head again, I asked him to sign the waiver in front of him that would affirm his decision and to hand it to my clerk.

As he started to write, a man stood up three rows back and said, "Your Honor, can I hire him a lawyer?"

I could have gaveled him out of order, but I like to allow a little leeway, especially since I recognized Brother Reuben and what were probably several of the Fayetteville mission regulars seated in the same row as the stranger. "Your name, sir?" I asked, motioning him forward.

"Jack Marcom, ma'am. From Brunswick, Georgia."

He was neatly dressed in pressed chinos and blue plaid shirt with a button-down collar. A pair of wire-rimmed sunglasses dangled from his shirt pocket. He held a blue canvas pork pie hat in his hands and the top of his head was nearly bald, making his long face look even longer. Midforties, I'd say. A couple of years younger than Buck Collins, but not quite as muscular.

"What's your relationship to Mr. Collins?" I asked, motioning him forward. "He's my wife's brother and I can get a lawyer for him if—

"No," said Collins, who had stood stolidly till then, not looking around when Marcom spoke. "I hold myself accountable and I don't want a lawyer, so let's just get this over with. Please, ma'am?"

"We will," I said. "But you're accused of a serious crime and I'd advise you to consider Mr. Marcom's offer."

"C'mon, Buck," his brother-in-law entreated. "Let me do this."

Collins finished signing the paper, gave it to my clerk and returned to the defendants' table, all without acknowledging the other man's presence.

"Can't I get him one anyhow?" Marcom asked me.

"No!" said Collins.

"Be seated, Mr. Marcom," I said. "Mr. Collins is the only one who can make that decision and if he chooses not to be represented, that's his right. Go ahead, Mr. Nance."

'This is a misdemeanor possession of stolen property, Your Honor," said Chester Nance, the ADA who was prosecuting today's calendar. "Also misdemeanor breaking and entering. Call Officer Walker to the stand."

The Dobbs police officer took the stand, was sworn in and stated his name and rank.

"Describe to the court what you observed last night around ten-fifteen," said Chester Nance.

In careful pedantic legalese, Officer Walker described how he was patrolling the town last night when he saw a man walking alone on the sidewalk outside First Baptist. Since downtown still rolls up the sidewalks at nine o'clock on a Monday night (my words, not Walker's), a pedestrian was unusual enough that he kept the man in sight in his rearview mirror.

"Then I saw him turn into the walk that goes around to the offices at the rear of the church. I drove around the corner, parked my cruiser, and came up through those bushes back there. I heard what sounded like breaking glass and arrived just in time to see the defendant reach through the door window, unlock the door from inside and turn the knob."

"And what did you do at that point?" asked Nance.

"I identified myself and placed him under arrest. Upon being searched, it was discovered that he had four credit cards which we ascertain to belong to four members of the church choir."

Nance held up a plastic bag with the multicolored cards, which he wished to place in evidence.

I took the bag and could read the names through the plastic. All were prominent, well-to-do women. I myself have never seen the point of having more than one credit card, but these women probably had stacks and wouldn't have noticed one missing card for days if Collins hadn't been caught. They were trusting souls to leave their purses in the robing room where anyone could get at them. Still, the only one I've ever seen carry a pocketbook with her choir robe is Miss Nora McBride, an elderly spinster who has an estimated worth of three million dollars and a soprano voice that soars like an angel's.

I handed the bag back to Chester Nance, who said, "No further questions, Your Honor."

I looked at the defendant. This close, I could see the flecks of gray in his beard and hair, the weathering of his skin. His eyes met mine, then dropped, as if in shame.

"Do you have any questions for this witness?" I asked him.

"No, ma'am. I just want to plead guilty and start serving my time."

I excused the witness. "Any priors, Mr. Nance?"

"Not in the state of North Carolina," said the ADA. "At least, not under this name. We haven't heard back from Georgia yet, and I have a feeling we're gonna find he's done this before."

At that point, Brother Reuben stood and raised his hand, "Ma'am? Judge? Can I speak on Brother Buck's behalf?"

"Very well. Step forward."

The preacher came up to the bar railing and said, "Judge, I know it looks bad, but this is a good man sitting here. Weren't you in that church Sunday morning?"

"I thought I remembered you," he said happily. "Well, if you were there, then you must a seen the goodness in his face, the sincerity in his voice—"

"But not the credit cards in his pocket," jibed Chester Nance.

"Now, I don't know how the devil managed to tempt Brother Buck," said Brother Reuben slipping deeper into earnestness, "but I do believe God told him it was wrong and I do believe God sent him there last night to put back that which he had stolen."

I looked at Collins. "Is that the way it happened?"

He nodded. "But I don't expect you to believe me and it doesn't really matter because I wasn't thinking straight. I see that now. I was trying to get away from this sin without paying the price."

Something about his mock-meek humility goaded me. "Tell me something," I said. "Just how many times have you done this before?"

"Done what?"

"Used men like Brother Reuben here to take you into affluent churches where you can find opportunities to steal? When they trace back on you, are they going to find a trail of missing credit cards or other items?"

He tried to meet my eyes and failed miserably. I was ready to give Collins the maximum sentence then and there, but the reality was that whether or not he got any jail time would depend on whether he had any prior convictions.

"Will two days give you enough time to hear from Georgia?" I asked Nance. He nodded.

"Then bring him back in two days and I'll hear his plea and set the sentence."

"Could we post a bond for him?" asked Brother Reuben.

I looked at Nance, who shrugged. "I've got no problem with that."

"Very well," I said. "Bond is set at five hundred dollars. See the clerk downstairs."

Buck Collins was the last case on my docket and I signed a couple of forms for my clerk, looked over the calendar for tomorrow, read through some pending files, then called it a day.

As I came down the steps at the rear of the courthouse on my way to the parking lot, I found Collins's brother-in-law loading the Plexiglass cross into the back of a ten-year-old white Chevy pickup. With sunglasses covering the lines around his eyes and that blue canvas hat covering his bald spot, he looked ten years younger than he had in court. Lettering on the truck door let me know that Jack Marcom was the owner of Marcom's Cabinet Shop in Brunswick, Georgia—"Cabinets and Bookcases Our Specialty." Not all that prosperous, if you could judge by the age of the truck. I noted that his only jewelry was a cheap wristwatch and a plain gold wedding band. The men who were helping him tie the cross down had the pasty faces of recovering alcoholics.

In front of the truck was a shabby old Buick station wagon with two more men leaning against it, probably waiting for Brother Reuben to finish up with the bail bondsman and paperwork that would get Collins released from jail.

Marcom recognized me even though I was no longer wearing my black robe and he tipped his hat. "I want to thank you, ma'am, for letting Buck out on bail. It'd near 'bout kill my wife to hear her brother had to stay in jail."

"Is she up here with you?" I asked.

"No, ma'am. I was coming up to Florence, South Carolina this weekend to see about some walnut trees that blew down during that last hurricane. Good walnut's hard to come by. And Bonnie, that's my wife, Buck's sister? Anyhow, Bonnie said long as I was this far north, how 'bout I come on up and check on him. Make sure he's okay. She worries about him out on the road, so whenever I get the chance, I bring him some fresh clothes, new shoes, some of Bonnie's homemade fudge. She was hoping now that winter's coming on, maybe he's walked far enough north, that maybe I could swing him around, get him to walk south for a change."

"How did you know where to find him?"

"Oh, he called Friday morning. Calls collect most times. He's the only family Bonnie's got. Besides me and the kids, of course. She told him to call her every week even if he didn't have the money and he's pretty good about it."

Marcom's matter-of-factness took me aback. As a child of a cynical culture, I was both amused and offended by Brother Buck Collins's wacky zeal, a zeal that was probably sincere despite his thieving. But clearly Jack Marcom saw him as the much-loved brother of his much-loved wife and took his ministry very seriously.

I walked over to get a closer look at the bright red cross. "You know, I saw Mr. Collins a couple of years ago when I was in South Carolina," I said. "It was almost dark, but the cross was all lit up. Does it still have a light inside?"

"Here, let me show you," he said, with almost proprietary pride.

He tugged at a section just beneath the crossbar and it popped right off. I saw that it had been held in place by strip magnets glued to the inner surface and to the plastic section itself. Inside was a small lightbulb wired to some flashlight batteries. A slotted section just below that held a thick packet of the inspirational leaflets and Bible tracts that Brother Buck had distributed at our church on Sunday. I suppose since the cross was hollow, he could have used it as a rolling suitcase except that clothes would have blocked the light. As it was, the light couldn't reach the very bottom of the cross because of the section that housed the wheels. That's why it had seemed to float on Collins' shoulders and off the ground when I first saw it in the twilight.

Now that I was up close, I marveled at the workmanship that went into that cross. Instead of just butting the pieces together so that the raw edges were exposed, someone had carefully beveled all the edges so that the joints were almost invisible.

"Before he went on the road," I said, "was Brother Buck a cabinet-maker, too?"

Marcom gave a rueful laugh and shoved his blue hat to the back of his head. "Buck's a good man, Judge. Out here doing good for the Lord as the Lord leads him, but you give him any kind of a power tool and you're just asking for trouble."

"So you're the one who really built this?"

"Well, we all have to use the talents we have where we can, don't you think? Bonnie, she said it was the least we could do to help his mission. And it's been real educational, some of the places he's been, the people he's met. Why, Jimmy Carter stopped along the road one time and talked and prayed with him for over an hour. Can you imagine that? A president of the whole United States? And when Buck came through Pinehurst a couple of months ago, some millionaire let us stay in his guesthouse right on the golf course." Awe and modest pride were in his voice. "Treated us like we were just as good as anybody else, which is what the Bible tells us, of course, but some people—"

I didn't get to hear the rest of his story because I saw Brother Reuben and Buck Collins push open the courthouse door and start down the steps toward us. Talking to Jack Marcom about the cross was one thing, socializing with someone I'd soon be passing judgment on was quite another. As I moved away, I asked Marcom if he'd be in court on Friday.

He nodded. "With a lawyer, if Buck'll let me."

I stopped by Aunt Zell's to pick up a pair of slacks she'd hemmed for me. She and Uncle Ash were on their way out to supper and they invited me to join them, but I wanted to get home before dark and work on the perennial flower border I'd planted beside my new porch. The weeds were about to take it. As I drove out of Dobbs, I was not surprised to come upon that cross again. Highway 48 leads not only to my house, but on to Fayetteville as well. What did surprise me was that the cross was now lashed to the top of Brother Reuben's battered old station wagon and Buck Collins was in the front seat. Trailing along behind was Jack Marcom in his pickup, accompanied by a couple of the mission derelicts. Why wasn't Collins riding with him?

On Thursday morning, while signing some forms for ADA Chester Nance, I asked if the state of Georgia had come through with anything on Buck Collins.

"Nope. South Carolina says they detained him briefly on a misdemeanor theft, but had to turn him loose for lack of evidence."

"That wouldn't have been at Broward's Rock, by any chance, would it?" I asked.

"Nope," said Chester. "Charleston."

I knew it would be a major and thoroughly unlikely coincidence and it was certainly a hair or two out of line as presiding judge. Nevertheless, at lunchtime,

I called my friend Annie and caught her at her bookstore. She remembered Buck Collins and his red Plexiglass cross perfectly.

"That's when Laurel's diamond earrings went missing from the choir room."

Annie's mother-in-law is a true eccentric who's prone to sudden enthusiasms, but I'd never heard that singing in a church choir was one of them.

"Oh, yes," Annie said grimly. "Two contraltos were out that morning and Laurel insisted on filling in for both of them. At the last minute, she decided that diamonds didn't go with her robe and she just pulled them off and put them in her purse and never once thought that the purse might not be safe there."

"Was Brother Buck in the choir room?"

"Yes, and we'd already had opening prayer and the first hymn before he joined the services. Laurel didn't notice her earrings were missing till we were on our way to Sunday brunch. We raced right back to the church and searched it thoroughly, but no luck. They weren't insured, either. That's when she noticed one of her credit cards was missing. We called some of the other choir members and they had missing credit cards, too."

The upshot was, Annie told me, that her husband Max rounded up their local police chief and took a speed boat across the channel. "When they got off the ferry, Max and the chief were waiting for them."

"Them?"

"His brother was with him that morning. I think he'd brought Buck Collins some new shoes. The old ones were worn out."

"So did they find anything?"

"Not a thing. The earrings were a matched pair of flawless diamonds, one carat each, but small enough to be hidden somewhere maybe, but what with the credit cards, too …" Her voice trailed off uncertainly. "Collins insisted that they do a strip search on both of them and the Chief complied. He even checked to see that the heels of their shoes weren't hollowed out. And Max searched the cross himself. Did you know it's hollow and has a light inside?"

I told her I did.

"You know, Deborah, our church gets a lot of summer visitors and I didn't like wondering if one of them was the thief, but Buck Collins struck me as a very sincere man. I'd hate to think I was such a bad judge of character. And speaking of summer visitors, when are you coming back to see us? Laurel's talking about taking the LSATs and applying to law school."

I laughed and told her to wish her mother-in-law good luck for me.

But after I hung up, I had to shake my head at Annie's trusting nature. She always thought the best of everyone. Buck Collins might have radiated innocence and sincerity to her; to me, he just looked guilty and ashamed.

And well he should. I'm always a little cynical about reformed sinners who parade their redemption so publically. Bragging that the Lord provided for all his daily needs.

Right.

With a little help from whatever his sticky fingers could pick up. Even if they were fenced for only ten percent of their actual value, two carats of flawless diamonds would pay for a lot of flashlight batteries. They would print a lot of Bible tracts. Not to mention a few religious T-shirts.

I thought of his sister down there in Brunswick. Another trusting soul, who helped the Lord provide, sending him shoes and homemade fudge. Least he could have done was give her a little credit.

Fudge? Shoes? Buck Collins had been on the road five years he said. That added up to a whole bunch of shoes. And probably warm jackets for the winter, not to mention underwear and jeans. Of course, the missions he stayed at could have provided some of his clothing, but I was willing to bet that every time he called home (and called collect, let us not forget), sister Bonnie was in his ear with "What do you need?" and "What can I send you?" then sending her patient and loving husband out five or six times a year to find him.

It was a wonder the poor man had time to keep his business going. And not going too well if I could judge by his old truck, his simple clothes, and the fact that his only jewelry was a cheap wristwatch and a plain gold band.

So maybe Buck Collins was right. The Lord had indeed provided by providing him with a devoted sister and generous brother-in-law. But here in Colleton County was where this Buck stopped, I thought grimly. If Chester Nance couldn't turn up any prior convictions—and one count of littering was all it would take—then the most I could do would be to hit him with a hefty fine and put him on probation with some community service thrown in. Either way though, this conviction would show up the next time things went missing from a church robing room.

I sat in court that afternoon dispensing justice. Or trying to. A B+ student on his second marijuana possession. The two migrant laborers who'd tried to knife each other but now claimed to be the best of friends. The relentless woman who kept calling her neighbor at three in the morning just because his dog barked a little. ("A little?" the woman screamed. "A little? Let me tell you—") And all through it, like a refrain—shoes and fudge, fudge and shoes. I found myself thinking about love and wondering if it went both ways.

At the break, I sent a note to Chester Nance, asking him to make sure the cross was in my courtroom the next morning.

So there it was, a fourth—and I hoped final—time. My bailiff propped it in the jury box, which was pretty appropriate. Brother Reuben and Jack Marcom were there once again to lend moral support as Buck Collins took his place at the defendant's table. Today's T-shirt was dark green with a scattering of flowers and the words, "Consider the lilies of the field."

"Have you changed your mind about an attorney?" I asked, when Chester Nance finished reporting that he could find no prior convictions of any misdemeanor or felony on Collins.

"No, ma'am."

"Mr. Collins," I said, "you are not under oath, but it's my job to ascertain the truth and I hope you will give it."

He looked at me warily.

"Did you take those credit cards?"

"I do plead guilty, Your Honor."

"That's not what I asked, Mr. Collins. Did you personally take those cards out of their purses Sunday morning?"

"It was a temptation too strong to resist. I am guilty."

I had to admire his wiliness. In another time, another place, he might have made a great trial lawyer.

"Yes or no, Mr. Collins. Did you take those cards?"

"Yes!" he said, almost exploding. "Yes, I took them, okay? There's a place I know that buys credit cards if you can get them there within twelve hours."

"Which you were prepared to do?"

"Yes, ma'am."

"And this isn't really the first time, either, is it? You took a pair of diamond earrings down in South Carolina, didn't you?"

"They searched me," he said. Behind the neatly trimmed beard, his face blazed red with embarrassment. "They didn't find them."

"Because you'd hidden them in the cross?" I asked.

"They looked there, too."

"Did they look in the secret compartment?"

He gaped at me. "How do you know about that?"

I directed the bailiff to bring the cross to him.

"It's in the wheel housing, isn't it?" I said. "You want to show me?"

With a sigh, Collins pulled off the magnetized strip of red plastic that allowed access to the wheel axle. Then he pulled at the inner plate that appeared to separate the housing from the hollow interior so that the leaflets couldn't fall down into the wheels and jam them. Instead the real separator, a rectangle of white plastic that didn't match the rest, was another four inches higher up, forming a neat little cubby hole plenty big enough to hold earrings or credit cards or maybe even a small kitchen sink.

"This is where I hid them," said Collins.

"You built it specifically to have a place to stash stolen goods?" I asked.

"Yes, ma'am."

"Oh, shoot, Buck!" said Jack Marcom on the front row behind him. "I already told her you barely know which way's up on circular saw. She knows you didn't build that."

"You be quiet, Jack!" He whirled around and shook his finger in his brother-in-law's face. "You just be quiet, you hear?"

He turned back to me. "I said I was guilty. What more do you need?"

"The truth, Mr. Collins. And in your case, the truth will set you free. As Mr. Marcom says, I have heard about your incompetence with tools. And this place that buys credit cards if you get them there within twelve hours? Carrying a cross, you could barely get out of Colleton County in twelve hours.

"You call home every Friday and tell your sister where you are and what you'll be doing. And if it's hanging out in someone's guesthouse by the eighth green or preaching to the well-to-do, then your brother-in-law shows up with fresh clothes, new shoes or food, doesn't he?"

"Bonnie and Jack, they believe in what I'm doing," said Collins.

"Did you ever think how expensive it must get for them?" I asked. "All those collect calls? How many children do your sister and Mr. Marcom have?"

He sighed. "Four."

I looked over at Marcom. "Four children to feed and clothe on top of helping your wife's brother, Mr. Marcom. When did you add that little box over the wheel housing and when did Mr. Collins finally stumble on it? Monday? Did he catch you retrieving those credit cards he tried to return that night?"

"He didn't know anything about it," Collins said stubbornly. "I had somebody in Charleston fix it for me."

Jack Marcom stood up, twisting his hat in his hands. "Your Honor—"

"You be quiet, Jack!" Collins roared. Then his voice softened. "You think about Bonnie and those little children depending on you and you just be quiet, you hear me?"

Marcom sat back down and Collins faced me resolutely.

"So what did you do?" Dwight asked me as we waited for the microwave popcorn to finish before sticking a video of *Stage Door* in my VCR.

(The ending's a little too schmaltzy for both of us, but we like seeing Lucille Ball before she became Lucy, and watching Katharine Hepburn come to terms with "the calla lilies are in bloom again" is always fun.).

"What *could* I do?" I said. "Without any priors, the law only allows a fine and community service."

I tore open the popcorn bag. The buttery aroma immediately filled the kitchen.

"But what about his brother-in-law? He might've been stealing from the rich to give to the poor, but he was still a thief and you let him off?"

"I didn't let him off," I said, nettled. "Collins let him off by swearing he did it all by himself. My only consolation is that if there's a next time, this will show up on his record."

"If there's a next time?" Dwight asked cynically.

"If," I said firmly. "I have a feeling Brother Buck had his eyes opened this week and that he really is going to trust the Lord to provide from now on, instead of his sister and brother-in-law."

"A fully reformed, reformed sinner," Dwight teased. "And all because of you."

I was still uncomfortable with the whole situation—punishing the technically innocent while the technically guilty went free? And yet, there was a certain rough justice at work here, though I never would have admitted it. And Brother Buck and Jack Marcom had each received a lesson in sacrificial love. All the same ...

"This isn't the way it should have turned out," I mourned.

Dwight patted my shoulder. "Well, now, you don't know that, Deborah. The Bible does say that the Lord works in mysterious ways."

"Maybe," I said. "I just wish He wouldn't do it in my courtroom."

— *Women Before the Bench*, Berkley, 2001

To celebrate their 25th anniversary, my publisher asked several of its authors to write a short story. We could write about anything we wanted as long as an anniversary was mentioned. I chose the 400th anniversary of Romeo and Juliet's opening night. Chronologically, it falls between Storm Track *and* Uncommon Clay.

WHAT'S IN A NAME?

It was a *Romeo and Juliet* love story.

Literally.

The Possum Creek Players staged a farcical version of Shakespeare's classic play last year—and yes, I agree that Shakespeare shouldn't be subjected to the desecrations of modern slang and modern levels of morality, but this was a very witty adaptation written to celebrate the four hundredth anniversary of the play's original performance. Although the first half was played for laughs, the direction was such that by the end, we had segued fully into the original version, language and all. The audience, which had come for the laughs, found themselves totally involved, and there wasn't a dry eye in the house when Juliet, arising from her drugged "death" to find that Romeo has killed himself, commits suicide herself.

No laughs. Pure Shakespeare.

Romeo and Juliet were played by a couple of semi-professionals with Equity cards, but the rest of the cast was drawn from stagestruck amateurs around the area. I myself played Lady Capulet, and before you picture me in gray wig and greasepaint wrinkles, remember that she was only fourteen when Juliet was born if you can believe the lines Shakespeare has her speak. Friar Laurence was played by Paul Archdale, a Dobbs attorney with a thick shock of white hair; and Marian Wilder, who owns a boarding stable between Dobbs and Cotton Grove, played Juliet's nurse.

It was lust at first sight.

But this *is* the Bible Belt and while the belt may have loosened a bit over the last few years, single women still can't let it all hang out. Not when they give riding lessons to impressionable children with straitlaced mothers. Nevertheless, courthouse gossip had Marian's little green pickup nosed under his carport, flank to flank with his silver BMW, six nights out of seven. His golden retriever immediately bonded with her fox terrier and the two dogs could be seen riding in her truck or romping together in the pasture almost every day.

Paul's taste usually runs to entry-level paralegals in flowery dresses, but he seemed to enjoy the novelty of a roll in the hay with someone who pitches hay for a living and who was his own age for a change.

Marian Wilder is widowed and childless and a lovely earthy woman with a heart as big as one of her horses. She wears her dark wavy hair clipped short and is letting it go gray. Her strong chin and determined nose are softened by deep blue eyes rimmed in long sooty lashes. Her laugh bubbles up in her throat like a brook that chuckles over smooth stones. It was clear to me what Paul saw in her, but I couldn't understand what she saw in him. He's a showboating egotist who never met a mirror he didn't love. It's impossible for him to pass any reflective surface without checking to see that his silk tie is perfectly knotted or to smooth his prematurely white hair with a beautifully manicured hand.

Marian cuts her own hair, probably hasn't had a manicure in twenty years, and prefers denim to silk.

With Paul's short attention span and voracious appetite, I expected the novelty to wear off before we finished rehearsals. But no, a month after we closed the play, I heard that he had been seen pricing diamonds at the Jewel Chest on North Main. My friend Portland, whose law offices are in the same building as Paul's, said he'd even asked her where she and Avery went on their honeymoon.

"You think it's possible Paul Archdale could love somebody besides himself?" she asked doubtfully.

"Do pigs fly?" I said. "Get real."

It came as no surprise when I heard that the affair had ended scarcely three months after it began. What *was* a surprise – and much snickered over behind Paul's well-tailored back – is that Marian was the one who did the dumping. It was a first for Paul, and not something he was treating as a life-enhancing learning experience, according to my sources (any resemblance between said sources and partners in his own firm being purely coincidental.)

None of this would have concerned me personally except that shortly after the breakup, Marian Wilder appeared in my courtroom before the first case was called. When I gave her permission to approach the bench, she came up, leaned in so that we wouldn't be overheard and begged me to sign a restraining order against Paul.

"He hurt you?" I asked, keeping my own voice low. "Threatened to kill you?"

"Not me," she said and her deep blue eyes filled with sudden tears. "June-bug."

The only Junebug in my memory banks was my brother Herman's grand-daughter, born in the month of June and a real cutie, hence the nickname. I hardly thought Paul Archdale was any danger to a four-year-old living in Charlotte.

"His golden retriever," Marian explained. "He's going to have her put down."

"You want me to restrain him from having his own dog put to sleep?"

"He knows how much I love her and this is his way of getting back at me for ditching him."

It was too early in the morning and I'd had only two cups of coffee. "Let me get this straight. Paul's mad at you, so he's going to kill his own dog for revenge?"

"He doesn't give a flying flip about her." Marian spoke so sharply that my clerk looked up curiously from her computer screen and a couple of lawyers sitting in the jury box paused in their whispered conversation. She glared at them and they immediately dropped their eyes.

"She was a legacy from on old lady that he conned the same way he conned me."

In passionate whispers, Marian explained that Junebug had originally be-longed to an elderly client, to whom Paul was assigned when she outlived the senior partner in his firm. She and her late husband had met at Duke and the bulk of their fortune was in trust to the university, but as she grew older, the interest accumulated faster than she could spend it and she found herself with a spare hundred thousand or so that wasn't already earmarked. Widowed and childless, she had poured all her love into her pets, a couple of ancient cats and a golden retriever puppy; and when she developed congestive heart failure, it had distressed her that they might be left homeless. Enter Paul, who shared her distress and guess what? Damned if he didn't seem to love her pets almost as much as she did.

"I think Paul hoped she'd leave him a bundle outright, but instead, she made him their guardian and left him six thousand a year for as long as they lived. The two cats died before she did, but Junie was still a pup."

"He's going to put her down and give up six thousand a year?"

"He says that's just chump change for him these days. The real reason he's doing it is because he knows how much it'll hurt me. When he was begging me not to leave him, I made the mistake of saying that I'd already stayed two weeks longer than I would have because of Junie. She loves me more right now than she ever loved him. And why not? I took her out of that fenced-in yard. I let her romp all over my pastures and bridle trails. She and my dog are like litter mates. You can't let him kill her! Please?"

Her eyes filled again and a tear spilled over onto her neat blue chambray shirt.

"I'm surprised he found a vet that'll put a healthy dog down for no real reason." I said as I clicked on my laptop computer and started looking for case law and precedents.

"He says Junie bit him. That's the only way he can get Gene to agree to this."

"Gene Adams?" Dr. Gene Adams takes care of Hambone, my Aunt Zell's beagle and had, despite his basic shyness, played the Prince of Verona in our production of *Romeo and Juliet*.

Marian nodded. "I told Gene he had to be lying. Everybody knows how sweet-tempered goldens are. No way she's a biter, but Gene says there's nothing he can do about it. He says that if he won't put her to sleep, Paul's threatened to just shoot Junie himself. They're going to do it at four this afternoon."

I pulled up the text to North Carolina's cruelty to animals statute and rapidly scrolled through, skim-reading as I went. The gist was that should any person "maliciously torture, mutilate, maim, cruelly beat, disfigure, poison, or kill" an animal, that person would be guilty of a Class I felony. The word "maliciously" was defined as "an act committed intentionally and with malice or bad motive." Marian could swear on the Bible that these words exactly described Paul's true motive for killing his dog. Unfortunately, the law had several exemptions and one of them allowed "the lawful destruction of any animal for the purposes of protecting the public, other animals, property, or the public health."

Paul didn't have to prove that the dog had bitten him. His word was enough. The law doesn't try to understand *why* a dog bites; it only assigns liability when it does.

"I'm sorry," I told Marian. "Unless there's something in the original owner's will, there's no legal way to restrain him."

"The will?" she breathed, hope spreading across her face.

"If she was a resident of Colleton County, it'll be on file here at the courthouse," I said.

Marian gave me the woman's name and I told her I'd look it up during my lunch break.

"If there's nothing there, could you just talk to him?" she implored. "He respects you. I saw how he went out of his way to be nice to you during the play."

I was amused. For such a competent business woman, Marian Wilder could be extremely naive. Of course Paul Archdale was nice to me. Most attorneys are. Judges are supposed to be objective, their decisions unaffected by personalities. But judges are also human, and when a ruling for your client could literally go either way, best not to have been rude or disrespectful to the judge.

If Paul's dog were a pit bull or rottweiler, I might not have interfered. But this was a golden, for pete's sake, probably the least prone to biting in the whole canine family. Against my will, I heard myself say, "Okay. I'll talk to him."

Easier said than done as it turned out. Paul was supposed to try a case in front of me later that morning, but the charges against his client had been dropped and the hearing canceled.

Down in the county clerk's office, I found Louisa Ripley Ferncliff's emended will with no trouble and was bemused to see that she must have been smarter than Paul could have wished because she'd figured out a dog's average life expectancy and put a sunset clause into the bequest. It expired this very year.

How nice for him. Put a guilt trip on Marian when he was probably going to dump the dog anyway now that she was no longer worth six thousand a year to him.

I called over to his office and was told that he'd be out for the rest of the day. A machine answered his home phone. I left a message, but wasn't hopeful he'd get it in time.

Court finished at 3:40 and Marian was waiting for me in chambers.

"Was there anything in the will to stop him?" she asked.

"Sorry," I said.

"Well, what did he say when you talked to him?"

"I didn't," I told her. "I couldn't get in touch with him."

She looked aghast. "And they're going to do it in twenty minutes! You've got to come with me to Gene's. Talk him out it. Please?"

It was only six minutes across the river to Gene Adams' clinic. Marian was so agitated, I made her follow my car instead of tearing over through red lights. When we got there, Paul and Junebug were the only ones in the waiting room. As soon as she spotted Marian, that beautiful animal stood up and started wagging her tail happily. Paul had to double his hold on her leash to keep her from rushing over. Marian immediately knelt down beside her and started petting the dog, who nuzzled her with touching enthusiasm.

Paul seemed surprised to see me.

"You here to pick up an animal, Judge?" he asked, reaching out to shake my hand.

"Not exactly." I kept his hand in mine and said in my most coaxing tones, "I came to ask you to rethink what you're about to do. Is it really necessary to put this dog to sleep? I read Mrs. Ferncliff's will and I know the dog's annuity expires this year, so couldn't you just give her to Marian? Let her go live at the stable?"

"And maybe have her bite one of the children who go to ride there?" he asked with matching earnestness. "I'd have it on my conscience for life if one of those kids had to have stitches in its face."

"Goldens aren't natural biters," I argued. "Surely it was an aberration."

He hesitated. After all, I *am* a judge and he's an ambitious attorney.

Unfortunately, Marian picked that minute to look up from the dog. "Liar! She never bit you. You're only doing this because I dumped you."

Paul's lips tightened and he gave Junebug's leash a vicious tug just as Gene Adams opened the door to his examining room.

The dog yelped and looked at Paul reproachfully but he didn't notice.

"Sorry, Judge," he said. "But the only thing to do with a biter is put it down."

Oblivious to its fate, the condemned dog had gone back to nuzzling Marian's hand, tail thumping happily against the tiled floor. Marian was openly weeping now and Gene was clearly distressed by her unhappiness, yet was too shy to offer a consoling hug. Paul tried to look sad but I could see malice in his eyes when Gene said, "Are you sure this is really necessary, Paul?"

"The damn dog bit me. It's my public duty."

So he had read the statute, too.

"What are you going to do with her?" Marian asked. "Afterwards, I mean."

That was clearly something Paul hadn't given thought to.

"I can dispose of the body, if you wish," Gene offered. His words were for Paul, but his eyes were on Marian and I suddenly realized that Paul wasn't the only one who'd fallen for her during the run of our play.

"No!" Marian said fiercely. "Let me bury her out at the stable. She was so happy there. Please, Paul! You can't say no to this."

Actually, he probably would have had I not been standing there.

"If that's what you want, then of course," he said, as if bestowing an enormous favor.

The injection wasn't something I wanted to watch, but Marian dragged me inside. Gene rummaged through his file cabinet and came up empty-handed.

"I don't know where my secretary keeps the releases," he told Paul. "But here." He quickly scribbled some phrases onto a pad. "Just sign and date this and we'll get started."

Paul signed impatiently without reading, then stood back as Gene lifted Junebug onto a table and weighed her so he could compute the correct dosage.

While Marian scratched her ears and whispered sweet sad words of goodbye, he filled a syringe with pentobarbitol and inserted the needle so gently that Junebug didn't flinch. A few moments later, the dog gave a big sigh and lay down. Her eyes closed, her body relaxed, her breathing slowed. Quicker than I expected, Gene covered the dog's body with a disposable paper sheet.

"So how much do I owe you?" Paul asked, reaching for his wallet and bringing it back to a commercial transaction.

"Nothing," Gene answered brusquely. "I don't charge for putting an animal to sleep like this."

"Well, okay, then," said Paul. "Thanks."

There was a moment of awkwardness as he tried to figure out the protocol of leave-taking after an execution.

Gene ignored his outstretched hand. "One more thing, Archdale."

"Yeah?"

"If you decide to get another animal, find yourself a different vet."

Except for the lines Shakespeare had provided, none of us had ever heard this big shy man speak so forcefully. Paul glowered and left in a huff, but Marian reached out her hand and squeezed his.

"Thank you, Gene."

He turned bright pink and said, "I'll carry her out for you."

I followed them to the truck and Marian had him lay the body on the passenger seat in the cab.

As he closed the door, Gene gathered his nerve and said, "I'm finished here for the day. How about I come on out and dig her grave for you."

"You don't have to do that," Marian said.

"I want to."

"Okay, then. Thanks. And thank you, too, Deborah, for trying." With tears stinging her eyes again, she gave us both impulsive hugs and drove off toward her stable.

Well, I thought, looking at Gene's face, one good thing might yet come out of this unhappy little episode.

Less than a week passed before I heard that Gene had located another female golden for Marian through one of the breed's rescue shelters. Once again her terrier had someone to romp with and people began to wonder—okay, *I* wondered—if there might be wedding bells in their future.

"In the fall, " Gene admitted shyly when I carried Aunt Zell's beagle in for its booster shots a month after I'd watched him euthanize Junebug. "I guess Archdale did us a favor after all."

"It was good of you to go help her bury the dog," I said, imagining the bittersweetness of the moment. Digging the grave. Laying that poor animal to rest. "Where did y'all put her? In the pasture?" Then I remembered that Marian had a small pet cemetery where her first pony was buried. "Or down by the paddock?"

Hambone yelped as the needle went in and it was a moment before Gene answered. "Under that oak tree at the top of her pasture. We like to ride up there."

"That's a beautiful view," I said, thinking that it was also a romantic view— rolling green pasture that sloped down to thick woods.

A week later, I found myself enjoying the same view while seated atop one of Marian's mares. I'd driven over that afternoon to ask what she charged for jumping lessons. One of my nieces wanted to learn the proper form and, since her birthday was coming up soon, I thought it might make a great present.

Marian was fuming because all the horses hadn't been exercised and when I showed up in jeans and sneakers, she soon had me booted and in the saddle of a sturdy little dun-colored mare named Cornelia.

She didn't look at all like my idea of a stately Roman matron.

"Her name was Cornmeal when I bought her," said Marian. "Horses and dogs. They know their names and if you want to change it, you have to pick something that sounds similar. Cornelia's maybe a little too elegant but Cornmeal was too much of a put-down."

We spent the next half-hour galloping briskly around the pasture. Tuggle, the fox terrier and Juliet, the new golden retriever tagged along till Marian blew on a dog whistle strung around her neck and with a gesture of her arm, sent them to wait for us on the crest of the hill.

"Juliet?" I teased when we pulled up beside them under that big shady oak. "Because the play was where Gene fell for you?"

"And I was so stupid I never noticed him for Paul."

"Don't beat up on yourself," I said. "You weren't the first, you won't be the last."

I glanced around, half expecting to see a stone marker, but the grass was smooth here under the tree. Nor was there any sign of recent digging.

"Where did you and Gene bury Junebug?" I asked.

"Down by the paddock," she said. "Next to Starfire."

I suddenly found myself remembering the apocryphal story of Susannah and the lying elders.

"We saw her sin under a mastic tree," the first one told Daniel when questioned separately.

"Under an evergreen oak," said the other.

"Ready for another gallop?" Marian asked, gathering up her reins

"Not just yet." I hadn't quite finished working it all out, but when I did, I laughed out loud, wondering just what sort of release Gene had maneuvered Paul into signing.

"What?" she asked.

"*What's in a name?*" I quoted happily. "*That which we call a rose, by any other name would smell as sweet,* right, Junebug?"

The golden retriever perked up her ears.

Marian gave me a wary look and her horse moved uneasily beneath her. "What are you talking about?"

"Shakespeare, of course. Juliet took a sleeping potion that, how does it go? ... *wrought on her the form of death*? Gene gave the dog just enough sedative to put her in a deep sleep and keep her asleep till he could be here with you when she woke up."

Her face paled beneath its tan. "He couldn't bear to let an animal be killed for spite. You're not going to tell Paul, are you?"

"Tell him what? That you have a new dog? When everyone's heard how much trouble Gene took to find you a dog as near like Junebug as he could?"

She relaxed visibly into the saddle. "Thanks, Deborah."

Down at the stables, an old blue Volvo wagon had pulled into the drive. Both dogs went streaking down the slope, racing to get to Gene Adams first.

Marian cantered after them, her face aglow with quiet happiness.

I chucked Cornelia's reins and we followed more slowly so that Marian would have time to warn Gene that I knew and to assure him their secret was safe with me.

Except that it wasn't. The very next day, Paul Archdale waylaid me after court. He stormed into the office I was using and acted ill as a cat with a tail full of sandspurs.

"I guess you and those two lovebirds think all golden retrievers look alike to me," he snarled. He was too angry to accord me the usual courtesy of my robe.

I closed the door and looked at him coldly. "I don't know what you're talking about."

"Marian was in town today and my dog was riding in the back of her truck. Adams never put it down, did he? And you were in on that little farce, too, weren't you? Begging to save it when you knew damn well Adams was just going through the motions to fool me."

"I believe you signed a paper giving him the right to treat the dog as he saw fit," I said, hedging for time.

A worthless ploy. No attorney worth his salt would let a little technicality like that deter him.

"He deliberately misled me." Paul's face was almost beet red beneath his thick white hair. There was nothing handsome about his mouth, now twisted with fury. "By God, I'll have his license and I'll have you up on ethics and I'll damn well see my dog with a bullet through its head before this day's out."

I could only stare at him impotently. While I could truthfully say that I thought Junebug was dead when Gene put her body on the seat of Marian's truck, there was no way I could put my hand on a Bible and swear I still thought she was dead.

Paul was almost bouncing on the balls of his feet in malicious triumph. "Thought you could fool me. Thought I wouldn't know my own dog!"

Well, as a matter of fact, yes. To most people, one golden retriever *does* look pretty much like another. Who'd have guessed that Paul Archdale had taken that much notice of a dog he'd never bonded with?

I thought of Gene Adams hauled up before a professional board of ethics. I pictured the very real possibility of getting censured myself.

And poor old Junebug. Finally free to romp and race and—

Hey, wait a minute here!

"I'm afraid you've made a mistake," I said. "It's not your dog."

"Like hell it's not!"

"No, no," I said, giving him my sweetest smile. "I read the will, remember? You and I are probably the only ones who realize it was probated seventeen years ago. There's no way that's the same dog that old Mrs. Ferncliff left in your care seventeen years ago. Marian's dog can't be more than three or four years old. But we'll get an opinion from an outside vet if you like. They can approximate an animal's age. An eighteen-year-old dog would barely be able to hobble across a room. It certainly wouldn't have the stamina to chase after horses all day. I'm sure the trustees over at Duke would be interested in learning just how long the original Junebug's actually been dead. Is this her first replacement or maybe the second or third? If we subpoena your financial records, will we find check stubs or credit card listings for the kennel where you bought them?"

I watched the color drain from his face as our roles reversed and he realized that he was awfully close to starring in his own ethics hearing. Not to mention a possible criminal trial if the Duke trustees did get wind of it and pushed for prosecution. I could almost see him multiplying six thousand dollars a year by eighteen years.

With compound interest.

I myself would need a calculator, but even without one, I knew it wasn't, to use his phrase, chump change.

"You're right," he said at last. "I was mistaken. It's not my dog." The words almost choked him. "I apologize."

As I watched Paul Archdale slink away like the villain in a Possum Creek melodrama, I couldn't help thinking of good old Shakespeare. An apt phrase for every situation.

Like, *all's well that ends well.*

—*The Mysterious Press Anniversary Anthology.* Mysterious Press, 2001

This story actually began as I've written it when I decided to do another circuit of our evening walk and my husband said, "If you don't come back, I'll send the dogs." We did not currently own a dog (his choice) so I laughed and said, "I'm tempted to stay out and see just what kind of dogs you'd send." But as I walked away into the twilight, I thought, What if I didn't come back? What if I vanished? This story almost plotted itself at that point. Chronologically, it falls between Storm Track *and* Uncommon Clay.

THE DOG THAT DIDN'T BARK

Feel like another round?" Donna asked as she and her husband neared the lane that wound through a stand of tall and bushy cedar trees and led to their back terrace.

Their lot here in central North Carolina was less than five acres, but she had mowed a long path though the property, a sort of lazy-eight shape that meandered though woods and field. It was more than wide enough for two people to walk side by side. Three times around was exactly one mile, and walking that mile with two-pound wrist and ankle weights was usually all that James felt like doing now that he was retired—especially in this muggy August weather to which his northern-bred body stubbornly refused to adapt.

"No, I think I'll go on in and make our drinks." Their regular evening walks were for physical health. Their regular evening cocktails maintained their mental health. "You go ahead, though, if you like."

"Maybe I'll just zip around one more time," said Donna, who had barely broken a sweat. There was a radiance about her lately, as if she'd discovered the fountain of youth since their move from northern Pennsylvania.

The setting sun cast long shadows around them.

"If you don't come back soon, I'll send the dogs."

She laughed. "I'm almost tempted to stay out till you do. Just to see what kind of dogs you'd send."

"What did she mean by that?" asked Major Dwight Bryant of the Colleton County Sheriff's Department.

"It was a joke," said Greggson. "You know—like, send the Marines? I don't care much for dogs and we've never had any, although she thinks we really ought to now that we're living in the country."

Country was a relative term, thought Dwight. The lots might be big out here, with tall leafy oaks and maples spreading deep shade around the houses and natural tangles of kudzu, honeysuckle, and cedars left along the road fronts to maintain the illusion, but they were still lots, not unbroken countryside.

"And you say that was about seven-thirty?"

It was now almost midnight, more than four hours since Donna Greggson disappeared. Normally they would have waited twenty-four hours before searching for an adult, but it was a slow evening and Dwight had been nearby when the call came in that a woman was missing—a beautiful woman somewhat younger than her husband, judging by the snapshots he'd seen. She had wide brown eyes, soft brown hair, and a teasing smile. At the moment, there were no smiles here in the Greggson living room, only anxious concern as her husband and their three nearest neighbors answered his questions.

Once, thought Dwight, he would have known all the faces living in this end of the county by sight if not by name. But there had been so much development over here in the last few years that the people in this room were total strangers to him.

He had learned that Mr. and Mrs. Zukowski were neighbors to the east and that Walter Malindorf's property touched both pieces at the rear. Like James Greggson, the other three looked to be in their mid to late fifties. Mrs. Zukowski—Marita—was tall and lean, with a strong-willed chin and the sturdy air of an outdoors person. Her husband Hank was lanky and thin faced under a thick crop of rusty brown hair. He had the kind of boyish good looks that ages well. Time would be kinder to him than to his wife, thought Dwight.

Malindorf, on the other hand, reminded him of a bantam rooster, loud and puffed with the self-importance that came from owning the largest "farmette" in this upscale development. Texans had a phrase for people who bought a sliver of earth and acted as if they held tide to a kingdom, thought Dwight: All hat, no cattle. In Walter Malindorf's case, it was all car, no crops. Shorter than the others by five or six inches and chubby where they were slim and fit, the man owned one of those outsized all-terrain SUV's. When Greggson called to ask if his wife was there, Malindorf had immediately come roaring through the wide mowed paths, shining his four headlights and side-mounted spotlight deep into the woods and across the open meadow, effectively destroying any physical traces that might have helped them determine what happened to the missing woman.

"Now you see here, Bryant," Malindorf blustered, his round face flushed with annoyance. "If she'd been lying out there hurt, you'd have been glad enough to have me find her pretty quick."

"But you didn't, did you?" said Hank Zukowski. "And now you've messed it up good for them."

Malindorf's red face turned even redder and he glared at his neighbor, rising on the balls of his feet to get closer to Zukowski's face. "Yeah, and if you'd kept your eyes open when you walked over, maybe you'd have seen who was sneaking around the place. If there was anybody to see."

"It's too early to say who should've done what," Dwight said, holding up a placating hand as he turned to Greggson. "Was there anything out of the ordinary about your routine today? Any visitors, unusual phone calls?"

"Nothing," James Greggson said firmly. "We worked on the yard this morning. It was getting so hard to mow under some of the trees that I cut a lot of lower limbs. Donna hates the sound of the chainsaw so she went inside for that. We drove over to the clubhouse for lunch, then trimmed up some bushes this afternoon. No phone calls that she mentioned. The cleaning woman came yesterday, so there was no one else here today unless you count the Mexican that comes in every week. He mowed the lawn, finished up the pruning, and hauled all the limbs down to the bonfire, but I don't think Donna said five words to him the whole time."

"Bonfire?"

"Yeah. We're planning a big Halloween party and we've been piling up all our burnable stuff on it for the last six months. Zukowski and Malindorf, too. It's going to be huge."

Dwight wondered if they planned to get a burn permit or if they knew how quickly bonfires could get out of hand with just the least little breeze? Well, one thing about these big lots, a fire truck could get here before a carelessly set fire burned more than three or four of their own acres.

"What's the worker's name?"

"Rosie's all I know. I always pay him cash, so I've never needed his last name."

"Rosario Fuentes said Marita Zukowski helpfully. "He mucks out the stable for me. Lives in Cotton Grove."

Dwight made a note of the name. "Was he still here when you went for your evening walk?"

Greggson shook his head. "Left at five sharp. Said his kid was pitching in a Little League game. I remember when my sons were in Little League," he added, his voice suddenly wistful. "I never missed a game. It's great the way people assimilate, isn't it? Man can hardly speak English and his son will be as American as apple pie."

He gave a rueful smile. "Or should I say American as tacos and enchiladas?"

From the woods out back came the sharp bark of a dog. Dwight stepped to the heavy French doors and opened them. Even at midnight, the air outside was still hot and muggy. No breath of wind stirred. He stepped out onto the broad, multilevel cedar deck and the others followed.

"No luck, Major," one of them called. "The dog's just going around in circles. If she left the path, she wasn't walking. We stayed to the edge much as we could, but all them tire tracks—" There was the suggestion of a shrug in the officer's voice. "Maybe in the daylight we'll be able to see something."

"That's it?" asked Greggson.

Malindorf's face began to redden again. "You're quitting? Just like that?"

"If the dog couldn't find her, there's nothing more we can do out there tonight," said Dwight. "We'll be back by sunrise, though. I'll post an officer and I don't want anybody else crossing the area till we can take another look at it in the daylight."

Greggson turned to Hank Zukowski. "You sure you didn't see her, Hank? The way she was headed was over toward your side of the property."

"What's that supposed to mean?" Zukowski asked mildly, a frown wrinkling his youthful brow. "I've told you no a dozen times tonight."

Greggson gave an impatient flip of his hand and turned away but the taller Zukowski grabbed his shoulder.

"No! First Malindorf here and now you. If I'd seen Donna, don't you think I'd tell you?"

"Unless—?" said Malindorf, deliberately leaving the word to dangle accusingly. "Unless what? Christ! You think I had anything to do with her disappearance? I was with James here. You said it yourself, James. I got here about five minutes after you left her and I haven't been out of your sight since then. When the hell did I have time to do whatever you're thinking?"

Dwight watched the distraught husband shake his head in weary frustration. "Sorry, Hank. I don't know what I think. I just want her to come home."

Marita Zukowski glared at the other two men and put out a comforting hand to lead him back inside the house. Dwight followed.

"I'm sorry, Mr. Greggson, but I have to ask you. Is there any reason your wife would leave on her own? Any trouble here that maybe made her want to get away for a while?"

"Of course not!" Greggson's steel-gray hair had begun to thin across the top, but his voice was still as youthful and vigorous as his handsome face.

"Then why did you wait so long to start calling your neighbors?"

"I told you. I thought she was playing with me. About sending dogs. Hank and I were here talking about the book he brought back, not paying attention to the time. I just assumed she was over with Marita. That's why I walked home with Hank—so she wouldn't have to come back in the dark alone. Then Marita said she hadn't been there, and that's when I called Walter. They're the only people out here we know well enough for Donna to drop in on."

Dwight's people had already searched the house from attic to basement, paying special attention to the auxiliary freezer in the basement and to the trunks and boxes in the attic. James Greggson might indeed be a loving and worried husband, but every officer was experienced enough to know that when a spouse goes missing, the remaining spouse is often responsible. So they looked very carefully at every container and cubbyhole large enough to hold a small woman. They even unrolled the large tent and sleeping bags stored there from the years of wilderness camping with his sons and grandsons.

When they finished with the house, they had moved on to the "barn," a three-car garage with a guest loft above and storage spaces the size of horse stalls to the sides, all under a gambrel roof. Working barns in Colleton County tended to be sided in sheets of tin, but Dwight supposed the dark red paint looked more authentic to somebody from Pennsylvania.

"Her purse is still here," Marita Zukowski said now, pointing to a side table near the door.

The summer bag was a feminine froth of multicolored straw. A tangle of keys lay beside it.

They all watched as James Greggson opened it and pulled out a slim wallet. They saw cash in the bill compartment and credit cards neatly slotted.

"Anything missing?" asked Dwight.

"American Express. They're all here. Her driver's license, and medical insurance, too."

"So she didn't leave under her own steam," Malindorf said. "I knew it! Just because this piddly-assed excuse for a sheriff's department's giving up doesn't mean we have to. Come on, guys, let's get our flashlights and go find her."

Dwight rose to his full six-foot-three, topping Walter Malindorf's take-charge pomposity by a good ten inches. "You go blundering out there again, Mr. Malindorf, and I'll arrest you for trespassing on a crime scene."

"Crime scene?" Hank Zukowski looked shocked.

"Until proven otherwise," Dwight said grimly.

"But she may be hurt," said Greggson. "Bleeding."

"The dog would have found her." He hated having to speak so bluntly, but they'd done enough damage between them and he wasn't going to allow more if he could help it. "We'll get an early start in the morning. Maybe something will give us a clue."

At that, the others rose, too.

Marita Zukowski gave Greggson a neighborly hug as she left. "Try to get some sleep, James. It won't help Donna if you worry yourself into a breakdown."

Dwight heard Malindorf offer the Zukowskis a lift since they couldn't take the shortcut to their house, but would have to walk around by the road As the monstrous SUV roared away down the drive, he paused by a display of photographs atop a console table. Most were of children and young adults. "Your children?"

"Mine, yes," said Greggson. "This is a second marriage for both of us, but Donna never had children."

"Any of them in the area?"

Greggson shook his head. "No. All back in Pennsylvania. Carrie, my baby—" Here he touched the picture of a younger woman holding two little boys. "— her husband was almost transferred to the Research Triangle, but it fell through."

"I'm surprised you could leave them," said Dwight, thinking of his own son up in Virginia, a good four hours away.

"I didn't want to," he admitted. "Not really. But the winters there are hard and Donna's brother's here, so—oh, Lord! I forgot all about Phil. He's in Raleigh. I'd better call him."

When it was clear from the one-sided phone conversation that Greggson's brother-in-law hadn't heard from the missing woman, Dwight let himself out into the warm August night. He spoke to the officer he'd left on watch, then got in his patrol car.

The mosquitoes were wicked tonight. Even though Marita Zukowski had slipped one of Hank's long-sleeved cotton shirts on over her bare arms, one buzzed around her face and another bit her bare ankle.

Everything that could be said between them had been said by the time they reached their own front door and Hank had gone on up to their bedroom. She told him she was going to walk their dog but that was only an excuse to hurry back down their long drive before that deputy could go away thinking what she feared he must think.

Duncan was as sweet-tempered and patient as most golden retrievers, and he lay quietly at her feet as she waited. She slapped at the buzzing near her ear and wondered if mosquitoes bothered him. In the middle of that thought, the patrol car finally pulled out of the Greggson drive down the road and she stepped from the shadow of the trees so that his headlights washed over her and her dog.

Dwight slowed to a stop and lowered his window. "You wanted to talk to me, Mrs. Zukowski?"

"Yes." Her voice was as tight as the skin stretched across the bones of her face.

He cut his lights, got out of the car, and leaned against it to listen to what this tall thin woman wanted to say here in the darkness, away from the others.

"James and Walter. They're making it sound as if Hank had something to do with Donna's disappearance."

"Were they?"

"Don't play games, Major. It may suit you to let Walter Malindorf think you're a country bumpkin, but I read that piece in the paper about you a couple of years ago. Ex-Army Intelligence? They don't take just anybody. You heard what James and Walter were saying, all right."

The moon had long since set, but there was enough starlight for him to see the urgency in her eyes. "So?"

"So, I just want you to know there's nothing to it," she said. "Hank and I had a light supper about six-thirty and he walked over to return a book about an hour later, just as he and James told you. Donna's a flirt and a tease and maybe Hank had his head turned for a minute or two when they first moved here, and maybe he did kiss her a little longer than he should have last New Year's, but you can't blame Hank for that. She's very pretty, you know. Doesn't look a day over forty though I know for a fact that she's fifty-one. Small and cuddly, too," she added bitterly.

Small and cuddly women made some men feel even taller and more manly, thought Dwight. Whereas a wife this tall, this angular—?

"There was absolutely nothing more to it than that," said Mrs. Zukowski, "but when you asked if there'd been any trouble and James said no, I couldn't contradict him right there, could I?"

"They were still fighting over a New Year's Eve kiss? Eight months later?"

"No, no!" she said impatiently. "They fought, but not about Hank. It was about staying here. You see, Donna wheedled James into moving to North Carolina even though he didn't want to leave Pennsylvania. He misses his old friends, his children, going camping with his grandchildren. I think he even misses the snow. The bargain was that he'd give it a try for two years and then they'd move back if he really hated it. She was so sure he'd love it as much as the rest of us do."

"Do you?" He was genuinely curious about the influx of new people, of why they came, and whether they found what they hoped for.

"Oh, yes! I've wanted a horse of my own ever since I was a little girl and now I finally have two. That was the big draw for this development. All the boundary lines are bridle paths held in common by the association. We can ride for miles out here. And Hank can golf three hundred days a year if he wants. I can't say I'm crazy about your summer humidity, but it doesn't bother me as much as it bothers James."

"Mr. Greggson doesn't ride or golf?"

"That's not the point," said Marita Zukowski. "Donna made a bargain she had no intention of keeping. It was just a way to get him down here near her precious brother and away from his children. The two years are up at the end of October, but last week, when he told her he wanted to put the house on the market next month, she just laughed at him. Said he hadn't tried to adjust and that North Carolina was their home from now on. James was furious. Ask Walter. He was there. We could see how angry James was, yet he just turned away and walked into the house and poured us all another round of drinks." She hesitated. "Something else, though."

"Yes?" asked Dwight.

"They've only been married a few years. The Pennsylvania house was his. This house is in both their names and North Carolina's a no-fault state, isn't it? If James left her, he'd have to split his assets and there goes a big chunk of his grandchildren's inheritance."

And what about Mrs. Zukowski? mused Dwight on the drive back to Dobbs. No-fault divorce cuts both ways. Would she have to give up those long-wished-for horses if her husband and her neighbor really were having an affair and it led to two divorces?

Daybreak came 'way too early next morning, but Dwight Bryant kept his word and was back at the Greggson home before the sun was fully up.

James Greggson met him in the driveway with his brother-in-law Phil Crusher, a compactly built man with the same wide brown eyes as his sister.

'Tell Bryant what you told me," Greggson said, when introductions were over.

"C'mon, James. It really doesn't mean what you're thinking," the younger man protested.

"Tell me what, Mr. Crusher?"

"It's just a coincidence," he answered reluctantly. "Last week, when Donna came into town for lunch, we got to talking about some movie she'd watched the night before. I forget the name of it. Something about a man who decided to disappear? How he put together some secret cash, got new identity papers and just walked away from his old life? She said that it might be fun to try it, except that if she did, the hardest thing would be never again seeing people you did love. Like me. But it was nothing, Major Bryant. She was just making conversation."

"You're sure?"

"I was till James here—" His voice wavered with uncertainty. "I thought we were too close for that."

"Then where's her passport?" James demanded.

"What?" said Dwight.

"When Phil told me what she said, I went upstairs and looked in the desk drawer where we keep our passports. Hers is gone. We keep some extra cash on hand, and that's gone, too."

"How much extra cash you talking?" asked Dwight.

"Fifteen hundred, two thousand. It varies. But she could easily have another twelve or fourteen thousand squirreled away. She isn't extravagant and I don't question what she spends as long as the accounts aren't overdrawn at the end of the month."

Must be nice, thought Dwight, who was paying his son's orthodontia bills in addition to child support and hadn't had an extra hundred since the divorce, much less an extra thousand.

"I hate to be so blunt here, Mr. Greggson, but was your wife maybe seeing somebody else?"

"No!" he said angrily.

"Yes," said his brother-in-law.

Dwight and Greggson both stared at him.

Phil Crusher was clearly embarrassed but determined. "I'm sorry, James, but I think she was."

"Who?" they asked.

"I don't know. She just laughed when I called her on it, but I've seen her like that before. Happy. Excited. Running on adrenaline. Just like the time she started with you."

"I didn't know she was still married then," James said stiffly. "She told me she and her first husband were legally separated."

The brother's assertion opened up other possibilities, but Dwight wasn't going to jump to conclusions. First things first.

Together, he and his team walked every inch of the wide paths, beginning at the huge brush pile in the middle, where the looping paths crossed. It was going to be another hot day. The green leaves on yesterday's freshly-cut tree limbs were already wilted and limp and the sun had begun to bake the open meadow where flowering weeds grew head high.

Above them, in the hard blue sky, a helicopter sent out from one of the Raleigh news channels made noisy sweeps back and forth over the whole area. The trees were too thick to see beneath, but if Donna Greggson's body were lying in the open, they saw no sign of it.

They fanned out across the property six to eight feet apart.

Not even a stray cigarette butt beneath the trees.

As a last resort, they dismantled the bonfire pile limb by limb, until it became clear that nothing was there except brush, scrap lumber, cardboard, and easily burned bits of household furnishings. Among the castoffs were a perfectly useable oak captain's chair with only one broken rung, a stuffed dog that didn't look as if a child had ever played with it, old magazines that should have been recycled, and some threadbare cotton bath mats.

By this time, pudgy little Walter Malindorf had driven over in his bright red SUV with Hank Zukowski. Both men seemed anxious to help in any way they could and offered to repile the brush. They acted grateful for the work and toiled away under the hot August sun until Malindorf's shirt was wet with sweat and even Zukowski was breathing hard. Dwight had seen this reaction before. It was the male equivalent of bringing casseroles to a house of bereavement.

Greggson came down for a few minutes, his handsome face haggard and drawn, and he watched Zukowski with suspicious, resentful eyes before abruptly turning away and stalking back to the house.

"What's bugging him?" asked Zukowski uneasily.

Malindorf picked up the stuffed dog, a golden retriever made of silky plush, pulled a handkerchief from the pocket of his chino shorts, and wiped sweat that trickled down his round cheeks. "Donna's missing," he said, his voice heavy with sarcasm. "Or didn't you notice?"

Zukowski stared at him, then shrugged and threw a final limb on the pile. It was much taller than Malindorf, but with a sort of solemn dignity, he stood on tiptoe to set the little dog as high up as he could, as if to leave it standing guard.

When Dwight asked if his people could search their outbuildings, both men agreed. He really wanted to search the Zukowski home, but without a warrant, he doubted they'd allow it and not even his favorite judge would give him one without probable cause.

Since the Greggsons' path edged the communal bridle path between their property and Malindorf's, and since golf carts and occasional light trucks also used the bridle path as a short-cut to the development's golf course and club house, it was clear that Mrs. Greggson could easily have disappeared by that route, willingly or unwillingly.

"But you'd think the dog would have found her scent," argued one of the deputies.

"Not if she was in somebody's truck," said another

"Or on a horse," said a third.

As they broke for lunch, Deputy Mayleen Richards arrived with the first results of her electronic inquiries.

"No records of anything more serious than speeding tickets," she reported glumly. "All solid citizens with triple-A credit ratings—the men anyhow. Mrs. Zukowski and Mrs. Greggson haven't held paying jobs since they married."

In her voice was the disdain working women often have for women who don't have to.

"Any dirt from the cleaning woman?"

"Just the usual. If they fought, it wasn't in front of her."

"And Fuentes?" Dwight asked.

Her freckled face brightened. "I checked his alibi myself with my brother's son. Billy Jim's on the same team as the Fuentes boy, who's got a slider that falls off the edge of the earth according to Billy Jim. Their game started at six- thirty and the boy's daddy was there from the get-go."

If Greggson was correct about the time he last saw his wife, then he and Zukowski alibied each other. Except for their dogs, Malindorf and Marita Zukowski had been alone in their respective houses. Malindorf had no apparent motive though and if Marita Zukowski had gotten rid of the woman she feared as a rival, then she was a damned good actress with nerves of steel.

By mid-afternoon, there was nothing left for Dwight Bryant to do except face Donna Greggson's husband and brother and promise that they would continue to canvass the neighborhood and follow up any leads their APBs produced. If she had left of her own volition, then sooner or later, they'd probably hear from her.

He let them vent on him the frustration he himself was feeling and promised to keep in touch.

And that's where matters stood through the rest of a torrid August and an unusually hot September. On a drizzly and cooler day near the middle of October, Dwight Bryant got a phone call from James Greggson. Once more he had to tell the man that there was nothing new to report.

"Actually," said Greggson, "I called to tell you that I've sold the house. I'll be moving back to Pennsylvania next week. You have Phil's phone number and I'll send you my new one as soon as I know it."

Nothing in his tone accused the Colleton County Sheriff's Department of incompetence, but neither did it sound as if he ever expected Dwight to use the new number.

This was not his first unsolved missing person, thought Dwight, and it wouldn't be his last, but he kept feeling that somehow he'd messed up here, that there must have been one more thing that would have made all the difference if he'd only noticed in time.

The drizzle ended in the afternoon and cool westerly winds blew away all the gray clouds, giving a hint of the beautiful autumn weather to come. As Walter Malindorf stepped outside to give his three spaniels a run, the tubby little man smelled something odd. He followed his nose around the corner of his house and saw wisps of smoke lifting above the woods that separated his place from Greggson's. Curious, he opened the back of his SUV, let the dogs pile in, then drove through the woods, across the bridle trail, and onto the wide path Donna had kept mowed until she disappeared.

Tall weeds with small yellow aster-like flowers had grown up in the past two months. Soon, he thought sadly, there would be no sign that a path had ever been here, that a small brown-haired woman with laughing brown eyes had ever passed along it.

As the path curved to the crossing, he saw that a ring of tiny flames edged across the damp grass toward the brush pile in the middle. Greggson had set a backfire to keep the main fire in check when it kindled and was standing alertly with pitchfork and shovel to take care of any stray sparks.

Since Donna's disappearance, relations had been strained between the three neighbors. Malindorf knew that Greggson suspected Zukowski of sleeping with his wife. He also knew that Zukowski denied it. Having no desire to listen to either man's bitterness, Malindorf had avoided them both. He wouldn't even have known that Greggson had sold the place if Marita Zukowski hadn't mentioned it when he ran into her at the club a few days earlier.

He climbed down from the SUV, well aware that Greggson considered him a ridiculous figure for buying such a vehicle. It would never occur to Greggson that someone could so enjoy the companionship of dogs that he'd buy a van for their comfort rather than his own. Well, the man was leaving. Wouldn't hurt to maintain the facade a little longer.

"Help you with that?" he asked as the flames reached the bonfire and began to eat at the base.

"That's okay," said Greggson. "The rain this morning damped everything down and there's not enough wind to worry about. In fact, if you don't mind, I'd rather do this by myself."

To take away the suggestion of insult, he added, "Donna was looking forward to our Halloween party and burning this with the whole neighborhood around. This is sort of for her, you know?"

"Yeah, sure," said Malindorf. He started back to the SUV, then hesitated. "Where's the dog?"

"The what?"

"The stuffed dog. A toy golden retriever. I set it up there near the top the day after Donna went missing—when Zukowski and I restacked the pile. Remember?"

Greggson shrugged.

Heavy gray smoke began to billow up from the center as the fire encircled the base and climbed the sides, growing in intensity. The broken captain's chair now lay atop the bonfire, yet Malindorf distinctly remembered throwing it on before covering it with some heavy limbs. And that blue cardboard box was one of his own contributions. It had been stacked on the other side of the pile.

"You restacked the pile?" he asked curiously. "Why?"

The answer came to him immediately. "My God! She's in there, isn't she? You killed her and now you're burning her body!"

Greggson glared malevolently, then charged toward him with the pitchfork. Malindorf dodged, barely escaping the icepick-sharp tines, and the momentum of Greggson's lunge carried him through the charred grass circle. He caught himself just short of the roaring blaze, but the points of the pitchfork pierced the blue box. He tried to jerk it free and a tangle of burning limbs tumbled toward him.

He abandoned the pitchfork and grabbed the shovel, but when he turned for Malindorf, he saw the little man scramble into his SUV and lock the doors. Howling with rage, Greggson swung the shovel at the windshield. The glass spider-webbed beneath the blow yet did not break. The dogs inside barked furiously and leaped from seat to seat. Greggson barely heard as he swung again at the window on the driver's side.

Malindorf ducked automatically but when his head reappeared, he had a cell phone against his ear and Greggson saw his lips moving above the mouthpiece. At that, James Greggson slammed the window a final time, then dropped the shovel and ran unsteadily through the cedars toward his house.

The volunteer firemen got there first. By the time they quenched the fire, Dwight Bryant had arrived with several deputies. They entered the house cautiously, weapons drawn, and called out for Greggson to give himself up.

They were too late.

James Greggson had drawn his own weapon. They found his body on the bed. There was no note.

"But where did he hide her all that time?" asked Malindorf. It was several hours later and they stood on the flagstone terrace of his house to gaze across at the glare of portable floodlights that still illuminated the bonfire site. The spaniels lay at his feet, alert to his every move. "We looked. I looked. Your people looked. You even had a tracking dog."

That had puzzled Dwight, too, until he saw the heavy green nylon bag and the ropes that the West Colleton Fire Department volunteers had pulled from the center of the bonfire. The contents sickened them. It had been a very hot two months. But the bag and the ropes made him remember the six-man tent in Greggson's storeroom and that in turn reminded him of his Army survival training.

"He sealed her body in a couple of large plastic bags, which hid her scent from the dog, then he put her in the tent bag and hoisted her up into one of those bushy cedar trees. That's what you do to keep bears from getting your food if you're camping in the wilderness. Hang it from a high limb. He must have hung her against the trunk so that our eyes would pass right over another limb shape. People don't look up much when they're searching. We found the tree, by the way. Just off the path where they grow so thick. We spotted a pulley screwed high up in the trunk."

One of the spaniels came and laid its large head against Malindorf's knee. Absently, he scratched the silky ear. "So he had it all planned and lied about the time he last saw her?"

Dwight nodded. "It's a good thing you noticed he'd restacked the pile."

"The stuffed dog was gone."

"Observant of you."

"Not especially." Malindorf looked at him sadly. "I gave it to her. The week before she died. A stand-in for the registered pup I was going to buy her for a divorce present."

"Divorce?" Dwight said. "She and Zukowski really were having an affair?"

"You, too?" Malindorf's voice was sardonic. "Good old Hank Zukowski. Tall, handsome, good physique—the automatic suspect when Greggson realized Donna was in love with someone else. He thought Zukowski gave her the dog. That's why he threw it on the burn pile. Never dawned on either of them that she might be tired of tall handsome men whose egos need massaging. That she might be ready for someone who could make her laugh, who could adore her."

"You?" asked Dwight.

Grief and wonder shone in Walter Malindorf's chubby face.

"Me," he said and began to cry.

— *Ellery Queen's Mystery Magazine*, December 2002

Marilyn Wallace, writing as Maggie Bruce, asked if I would contribute a story that featured some sort of craft to her anthology Murder Most Crafty. *I thought perhaps Deborah could manage a grapevine wreath with a little help from her sisters-in-law. The story itself was inspired by a real New Year's Eve bonfire here on the farm when a cousin tried to burn some overly wet wood. When my brother said, "Never saw gasoline so wet it wouldn't burn," I knew I'd use that sentence in a story sometime. They really did try to chase some lovers out of that lane and yes, they really did get mired down to the axle. Chronologically, this falls between* Rituals of the Season *and* Winter's Child.

BEWREATHED

Okay, so I wasn't freezing in Times Square waiting for the big apple fall at the stroke of midnight. Nor was I in Raleigh waiting for the brass acorn to fall and listening to Dwight Bryant grumble about it being cold enough to freeze similar objects off brass monkeys.

Instead, I was standing on a rise overlooking my brother Robert's back fields watching Robert try to get a pile of stumps and scrap lumber— *soggy* scrap lumber I might add—to burn while four of my other brothers made helpful remarks like "Ain't you got no kerosene, Robert?" or "Didn't I see a can of gas under your tractor shelter last week?"

It wasn't even all that cold The night air was cool and damp, invigorating without winter's usual raw chill.

All the same, this wasn't how I'd visualized spending my first New Year's Eve with Dwight. We had talked about going to Raleigh's First Night celebration with some friends and I'd even bought tickets back before Christmas, then Dwight, who heads up Sheriff Bo Poole's detective squad, got caught short-handed with two deputies in bed with flu and a rash of break-ins across the county.

As a district court judge, I know first hand that crime doesn't take a holiday, but court does and I've always packed a lot of playtime in the week between Christmas and New Year's, so I was disappointed that Dwight couldn't come play, too. I gave the tickets to one of my nieces and was prepared to throw myself a solitary pity party when April called to see if they could borrow a suitcase. April teaches sixth grade and she and my brother Andrew were taking their kids to Disney World over the school break next week. As soon as she heard Dwight had to work, she insisted I come along with them to Robert's.

"You want a wreath, don't you?"

"So?"

"So Robert pruned his grapevines today and saved the cuttings for me." My sister-in-law is so creative she could probably knit a tree if she'd only slow down long enough to find the right yarn. "We'll build a bonfire, roast hot dogs, start you a wreath and see the New Year in together, all at the same time. Minnie and Seth are coming, Haywood and Isabel, Zach and Barbara, too," she said, naming others of my brothers and their wives who still live out here on the family farm along with her and Andrew. "Robert says Doris has even bought a bottle of champagne." (Despite France's battle to keep Champagne from becoming a generic term, here in Colleton County, any white wine that sparkles is automatically called champagne.)

I had to smile. "One bottle for a dozen people?"

"Well, you know Doris."

I did. Robert's the oldest of my daddy's eleven sons and his wife is one of the most conflicted hostesses I've ever seen. She truly wants to be generous but she can't help counting the cost—the heart of a bon vivant housed in the body of a miser.

"We're going to do a loaves and fishes on her," April said, laughter bubbling in her throat. "You got anything fizzy in your refrigerator?"

"Two bottles," I told her. "Count me in."

"Andrew says we'll pick you up around nine."

I called Dwight to let him know where I'd be in case he could get away before midnight. He was in and out of our house so much when we were growing up that he knows Robert and Doris about as well as I do and is equally amused by them. "At least I won't have to worry about you getting too much to drink," he said.

"Don't count on it," I said. "How's the surveillance going? Any sightings?"

"Nothing so far. I've got patrol units out all around Cotton Grove, but hell, Deb'rah, we're probably not going to hear about any break-ins till the owners get home to tell us."

With its easy commute to the Research Triangle, Colleton County's experienced such a population boom in the last few years that we now have our share of the usual misdemeanors, petty felonies, and yes, the burglars who would rather steal for a living than work.

From sitting in court, I've learned that their victims will often have a pretty good idea of who's ripped them off. It will be the friends of their teenage children, itinerant repairmen, or a pickup laborer who cased the place while cutting grass for the homeowner's lawn service.

Beginning at Thanksgiving though, there had been a systematic looting of eight or ten homes over the past few weeks and nobody had a clue. At each house, the owners were away for at least three or four days, either on vacation or traveling for business or pleasure during this holiday season. All were within the same five mile radius of where we live. All were without burglar alarms, in middle-class neighborhoods, and entry was always by breaking through a rear door or window. The only items taken were money, jewelry and small electronics that were easily fenced. So far there were no fingerprints and nothing to indicate whether it was the work of a single person or a whole gang. Trying to figure out how the perps knew which houses would be empty was driving Dwight crazy.

At first, he thought that dogs might be the link since the first four houses did shelter canine pets and all four had boarded their dogs in the same kennel. That theory went bust when the next three break-ins were at dogless homes.

Now people are often careless about the little things that will let a thief know if a house is empty. Mail will pile up in the mailbox, newspapers will litter the driveway once the box is too full to hold more. In summer, the grass will go uncut. Winter's a little harder to read since we seldom get enough snow to bother with shoveling the drives. But these latest victims had taken all the sensible precautions. They had stopped delivery of mail and newspapers, they used timers to turn lamps on and off at normal hours, they even alerted nearby neighbors to keep an eye out. Unfortunately, nothing seemed to be working.

"Could it be loose lips at the post office?" I had asked. "A mail carrier would know as soon as someone on the route suspends their mail."

Dwight reminded me that our area is serviced by two separate postal zones.

"Well, what about newspapers?"

"Same thing. Billy says that the *News and Observer* has at least three different carriers out in this part of the county." (Billy Yost is a neighborhood kid who's been delivering papers to the farm ever since he got his driver's license.) "Plus separate carriers for the local weeklies. He thinks that all told, we're looking at six or seven carriers at least. In fact, one of them's his grandmother's friend, Miss Baby Anderson; and you know good as me there's no way Miss Baby is part of any burglary ring."

"Good lord! Is she still delivering the Cotton Grove *Clarion*?" Miss Baby Anderson is a scrappy 82-year-old poor but proud grandmother who has always lived near poverty level.

"Every Tuesday afternoon," Dwight said. "I guess she needs to supplement her Social Security."

The Sheriff's Department had issued warnings through all the little weekly papers but Dwight fully expected to hear of several more incidents when people got back from their Christmas travels, and he wasn't looking forward to their unhappy complaints about poor crime control.

"Maybe you'll get lucky tonight," I told him.

"I certainly hope so," he said; and from the leer in his voice, I realized that we were no longer talking about his work.

"I'll save you some champagne," I promised.

So here I was on New Year's Eve at the edge of Robert's small vineyard, watching Robert try to get his bonfire started while Doris set out hotdogs, buns, chili and coleslaw on an ancient picnic table Robert had hauled out to the site. We'd had a rainy autumn, but these logs and boards looked as if they'd been dredged from a swamp the day before.

"Where the hell did you get this wood?" asked Zach, one of the "little twins" next up from me in age..

"Part of it's the old strip house the last hurricane knocked down, the rest are stumps out of that bottom land I drained this fall," Robert admitted.

He sloshed gasoline over the pile and lit another match. There was a brief splutter of flame, then nothing.

"First time I ever seen even gas too wet to burn," muttered Haywood, one of the "big twins."

My brother Seth dangled his truck keys out to Haywood's son Stevie, the only nephew to elect to see the New Year in with us rather than drive into Raleigh. "How 'bout you run fetch me my blowtorch?"

"I'll ride over with you," I said. Stevie's my favorite nephew and I hadn't seen much of him over the holidays. His girlfriend was off somewhere with her family and he was at loose ends this weekend, so this gave me a chance to ask how life was treating him.

Pretty fine," he said as we navigated the back lanes from Robert's part of the farm through a shortcut to Seth's workshop. Stevie and Gayle had been together since high school and would probably marry after they finished college.

"What about you? What's monogamy like?"

"You ought to know," I told him. "You've been monogamous a lot longer than I have."

He grinned. "That good, huh?"

"Yeah," I said happily as we rooted around in Seth's shop for his hand torch.

"So how come Dwight's not here tonight?"

I described the break-ins and how the sheriff's department was stretched thin with two deputies out sick. Like me, Stevie immediately suggested that Dwight should look at the people delivering the mail or the newspapers.

" 'Way ahead of you," I said. "Some of the burglaries were committed in the Cotton Grove postal zone, the others in the Dobbs zone. And Billy says there are several paper routes in this area."

"Billy Yost?"

"That's right, you and he were in school together, weren't you?"

"Before he flunked out. Life's not fair, is it, Deborah?"

"Never has been," I agreed.

"I mean, here I am, halfway through college and he's still delivering papers."

"Somebody has to."

"Yeah, but Billy's smart. Smarter than me. He shouldn't've had to work so hard that he couldn't stay awake in class."

We both spotted Seth's blowtorch at the same time, hanging from a nail on the side wall. When we were back in the truck, I said, "So if Billy was that smart, why didn't he just ride the schoolbus?"

"You think the only reason he worked three jobs was to support a car?"

"A lot of kids do."

"Not Billy. His grandmother raised him and she didn't have anything but Social Security to live on. He felt like he owed her. He used to say there wasn't enough money in the world to pay back the old women who step in and take over when their sorry children can't hold it together."

I remembered the details now—no father, abused by a mother on crack and whoever she was sleeping with at the moment—no wonder he'd want to repay his grandmother for taking him out of all that when he was six or seven.

"Speaking of old women, Dwight says Miss Baby's still delivering the *Clarion*," I said and Stevie shook his head as he maneuvered the truck around a fallen tree.

"North Carolina lets her drive? Isn't she about a hundred and ten now?"

Back at Robert's, a lopsided moon had risen over the treetops that rimmed his lower fields.

It was a week past full but still cast a cold blue light across the landscape. Through the far trees, a good quarter-mile away, we could see the streetlights of yet another new housing development. A light breeze blew up from the bottom, bringing a clean smell of damp earth and the promise of a new seedtime and new beginnings.

Using Seth's blowtorch and the rest of the gas in Robert's can, my brothers finally got the bonfire going and Doris kept urging us to take another little sip of her ersatz champagne.

"These bottles sure hold a lot, don't they?" she marveled.

By then, we had topped her bottle off at least twice without her noticing. She also hadn't tasted any difference between her $2.69 Food Lion bubbly, April's Corbel, or my Roederer Estate.

April had piled the grapevines on the back of their pickup and she sat on the tailgate to start coiling a wreath while the men scrounged for fallen limbs out in Robert's wood lot. My other sisters-in-law came over to watch.

"If these weren't freshly cut, I'd have to soak them overnight in warm water," April said as she gathered up several vines and began bending them into a circle. When the circle was as thick as her arm, she deftly wove the loose ends back onto themselves and soon had a nice tight wreath. I'm not into cutesy, but I thought a rustic grapevine wreath on our back door might get me a few points for domesticity, maybe keep people from feeling so sorry for Dwight. Securing the vine ends was harder than it looked and my wreath was nowhere near as tight as April's when I'd finished.

"If it starts to fall apart, you can just wire it back together or hit it with some hot glue," April said reassuringly. "What sort of theme you want?"

"Theme?"

"You know—winter? Spring?"

"Valentines," Doris teased; and Isabel said, "How about a pair of little turtledoves for you lovebirds?"

"Oh, please," I said.

Barbara laughed. "I have some wooden hearts and a can of red paint."

The bonfire was burning brightly now and they'd all had enough sips of sparkling wine to begin feeling a New Year's glow.

"Little gold cupids!"

"Lace and red foil!"

"Shiny packs of Trojans!"

"Forget it," I said firmly as the suggestions grew raunchier.

From beyond the fire, Robert suddenly called, "Hey! Who you reckon that is?"

We looked down the hillside to where he pointed. Off in the distance, car headlights swept through a cut in the woods that led from the road to his back lower fields. The lights shone straight across the bare land, then suddenly went dark. The moon wasn't quite bright enough to let us see the car, although we could hear the engine as it continued on course as if the driver knew exactly where he was going and the moon was all the light he needed.

Robert and Haywood immediately reverted to form. Ask a farmer for permission and he'll let you dig dogwoods and willow oaks out of his woods. He'll let you hunt rabbits or doves. He'll keep you in watermelons and sweet corn all summer, let you cut Christmas greenery in winter. But pick a single wildflower, shoot a single rabbit without asking, and he'll bristle up and invite you to get the hell off his land, often at the end of his shotgun.

"Come on, Haywood," Robert said, lumbering toward his Chevy pickup. "Let's go down and chase 'em!"

"Aw, now, honey," Doris protested. "What are they hurting?" Every one of us had parked down at the end of deserted farm paths in our time, and we murmured in agreement when Isabel said, "Oh, let 'em celebrate in peace."

Robert and Haywood were too bullheaded to listen though and they roared off together in Robert's pickup. Andrew, Seth and Zach just shook their heads and piled more limbs on the bonfire.

From our vantage point, we watched Robert's lurching headlights leave the lane and strike a diagonal across the field.

"I don't think that's a good idea," said Zach.

"It's okay," said Doris. "He's got four-wheel drive."

"Yeah, but the land's real low back there," said Seth.

Zach turned to Andrew. "Didn't one of the tractors bog down there last winter?"

Andrew nodded. "Took three others to pull it out."

I crawled up on top of the cab of Seth's truck and perched there cross-legged to enjoy the show. Sure enough, it wasn't long till we heard the high-pitched rrrr-rrhrr-rrrhrrr of spinning tires going nowhere fast, then the slamming of truck doors. A flashlight bobbled across the field as Haywood and Robert made their long muddy way back up the rise to us.

"I reckon we gave 'em a good scare though," Robert said smugly.

Haywood stomped the mud from his boots. "They probably slipped out while we was driving down there."

"I think they were further back," I called from atop Seth's cab.

"Naw, shug," said Robert. "I got four-wheel drive on my truck, and if *I* got stuck up to the axle, ain't no car could've gone further."

"Uh, Robert?" I pointed down behind him.

He whirled in time to see a glow in the far field resolve into car lights as it zoomed straight along the field's bottom lane, back through the woods and out toward the safety of the road.

"Well damn!" Robert said. Then he shrugged. "All the same, I bet that was the shortest loving *he* ever got."

"Spoilsport," said April.

"Never mind about them," said Doris. "That fire looks about ready, don't y'all think?"

We threaded bright red hot dogs on wire coat hangers that Robert had straightened out, and we held them in the bonfire till they were charred on the outside and warmed through the middle, then popped them into buns and spooned on the onions, chili and coleslaw. Even though Doris had bought the cheapest brand sold, everything combined to make those hot dogs taste like gourmet sausages.

It was ten minutes till twelve and I was fixing myself a second one when Dwight pulled in.

"Just in time!" Doris called to him happily and waved her heavy green bottle in his direction. "Still plenty of champagne here. Nobody seems to be drinking it but me."

All around the neighborhood, colorful bottle rockets shot up in the sky, and firecrackers popped as the old year wound down. Zach and Stevie set off a few fireworks of their own, and I gave Dwight my hotdog and a cup of the good stuff. Robert had his pocket watch out to count down the minutes, Andrew cranked his truck radio up so we could hear the announcer in Times Square, and all my brothers began to edge closer to their wives. Dwight set his hotdog down on a paper plate.

"Ten! Nine! Eight!" chanted the crowd from New York, and we joined in. "—four—three—two—one—Happy New Year!"

Dwight's kiss was long and satisfying. He smelled of woodsmoke, onions, champagne and aftershave and I could have taken him right there except that we were suddenly in the middle of an exuberant group hug with my brothers and sisters-in-law, who were tipsily singing "Auld Lang Syne." Somewhere in the distance an iron farm bell rang and more rockets exploded overhead in a cascade of bright sparks.

Dwight and I slept in the next morning and were finishing up a late breakfast when April came by to drop off my wreath. She and Andrew were on their way back to Robert's to help pull his truck out of the field. Dwight offered to help with a length of heavy chain. I wasn't going to stay home and miss the fun and besides, it would give me a chance to find stuff for my wreath.

Seth was already out in Robert's muddy field with one of the tractors when we got there; and while the men debated whether it was better to haul the truck out frontwards or backwards, April and I walked down the far lane to pick up gumballs. Sweetgums are a nice shade tree, but they shower down hundreds of prickly walnut-size seed balls every winter and make walking such a hazard that nobody lets them grow in the yard. We found clumps of silvery gray dried moss, hickory nuts and some small pine cones, too. Then, because our eyes were searching the ground for seed pods and other woodsy objects, we saw where that car last night had turned around. We also saw fresh shoeprints in the soft earth, prints that began at the car and disappeared through the hedgerow.

April giggled. "He must have had to answer a different call of nature."

"I don't think so," I said.

The hedgerow here backed up to the new development; and beyond the bare twigs and scraggly bushes, thin morning sunlight reflected off a broken rear window of the nearest house.

"Watch out where you walk," I told April. "That was no horny teenager last night."

"Good eyes," Dwight said after he went across to check on the house. It had definitely been broken into and no one seemed to be home. He called for the crime scene van to come out and record the tire and shoe prints we'd found, and he got the owner's name and holiday vacation phone number from a hungover neighbor across the street who was supposed to be keeping an eye on the place. "Who the hell expects somebody to break in on New Year's Eve?" the neighbor asked plaintively.

It didn't take Dwight long to learn that the mail was delivered by one of the Cotton Grove carriers, that the Raleigh daily paper was delivered by a reformed drunk named Sam Parrish, and that the *Courier* was delivered by "some sweet little old lady."

"Miss Baby Anderson?" they asked.

"That's her name," said the neighbor's wife. "I don't know how she keeps going, out driving in all sorts of bad weather. It's a wonder she's not been sick more this winter."

When Dwight told me that, I started thinking about Miss Baby. She was almost as poor as Billy Yost's grandmother, yet when I ran into her at the grocery store a week or so earlier, her basket had held a large rib roast— "Everybody's coming to my house for Christmas dinner," she'd said happily, "and they're tired of turkey so they've all chipped in."

"Sounds like you're going to have a big time," I said.

"Oh, we are." She beamed. "A real party. I'm even going to ask Sarah Jeffers and her boy to come eat with us, too. Billy's been so good to me, almost like another grandson, always bringing me little things he picks up at yard sales, taking on with my paper route whenever I was sick this winter. I owe that boy a lot."

Like Billy's grandmother, Miss Baby was another who had stepped in to help raise the children of her children. Her winter coat was old and frayed at the wrists, but when she reached out to pat my arm in parting, I had noticed that she wore an expensive designer gold watch.

Billy was so good to her?

"Let me see your checklist of stolen goods again," I told Dwight.

It was the second night of Andrew and April's vacation trip, the second night that Dwight and I had turned out their lights at ten-thirty and waited in their darkened living room. Normally, none of us bothers to stop our mail or newspapers because there's always a sibling willing to empty the boxes, but April had agreed to my plan and had made the necessary calls before they left.

Dwight thought that staking out their house was a waste of time. "Nobody who knows this neighborhood's going to rip off one of my brothers-in-law," he'd argued. "And even if they do, you shouldn't be here."

"It's my idea," I said stubbornly. "And my brother. And I don't care what Miss Baby was allowed to think. Her new watch didn't come out of any yard sale."

Reluctantly, Dwight had admitted that such a watch had indeed gone missing from one of the burgled houses.

We were snuggled together on the couch under one of April's patchwork quilts, my head in his lap, and both of us were half asleep when the sound of breaking glass brought us instantly to our feet. I grabbed the flashlight on the table and Dwight drew his gun.

We tiptoed down the hall and into the kitchen where we saw a slender figure silhouetted against the outside security light. A gloved hand reached through the broken door pane and turned the door knob. A wave of cold January air flowed over us.

As soon as the door opened and the burglar was all the way into the kitchen, I hit him with the light and Dwight said, "Game's over, Billy."

"Oh, dear!" said Miss Baby Anderson.

"Miss *Baby?*" asked April when we were telling her and Andrew about that night. "But we're not even on her route."

"No, but you're on Billy's," I said.

"Billy Yost and Miss Baby were working together?"

"Billy didn't have a clue," said Dwight. "His car tires didn't match the casts we made in Robert's field the other day, but we still thought he was our perp because Deborah noticed that he or Miss Baby one delivered to every house that was hit."

"She and Billy's grandmother are close friends," I said, "so I asked around and learned that whenever she was sick this winter, Billy would fill in for her. That's why I was so sure he'd know her schedule and know when she'd been told not to deliver the *Clarion.*"

"Instead, it was the other way around," said Dwight. "He kept a copy of his schedule on the refrigerator so his grandmother would always know where he was if she needed him in an emergency. Miss Baby started checking it out whenever she was over there, noting down which houses would be empty and easy for her to break into."

"But why?" April asked.

We could only repeat what Miss Baby had told us while we waited for a squad car to arrive. The watch was the one piece of jewelry she'd kept. The rest had been fenced for food, medicine and small luxuries.

"I've worked hard and lived poor my whole life and I was flat-out tired of doing without," she'd said. "Then my heart pills went up again right before Thanksgiving, and that was the last straw."

Her belligerent attitude had taken me by surprise, but I was cynical enough to know that by the time her case came to court, she would again be a sweet-faced, silver-haired little grandmother who would tug at a jury's heartstrings and earn herself a suspended sentence. Zack Young would probably defend her *pro bono* and I could see a defense based on the high cost of prescription drugs so that the country's whole health care system would be on trial, not just Miss Baby.

As we stood to go, I asked April if I could borrow her glue gun to finish my wreath.

"Sorry," she said. "I lent it to Doris this morning. She and Isabel and Barbara are working on something."

Two days later, when Dwight and I got home from work, we discovered what that something was. An enormous heart-shaped wreath hung on our back door. It had been wrapped in black and white ribbons to look like a convict's striped uniform. Hot-glued to it were a couple of toy pistols, some star-shaped sheriff's badges from Bo Poole's last election campaign, and a small wooden gavel. A pair of toy handcuffs dangled from the bottom of the wreath and each cuff framed a picture—one of Dwight, one of me. White letters had been glued to the black ribbon stretched across the front: "Life w/o Parole."

Dwight grinned.

"Works for me," he said.

— *Murder Most Crafty,* Berkeley Publishing Group, 2005

Chronologically, this story falls between The Buzzard Table *and* Designated Daughter.

BY A HAIR

According to the clock by our bedside, I had been asleep less than two hours when I was awakened by my husband pushing back the sheet that covered us as he sat up in bed, alert to the sound of sirens shrieking down one of the roads that border our family farm.

"Dwight?" I said. "Where—?"

He held up his hand for silence so that he could get a better fix on the sirens that suddenly quit blaring as he reached for his pants.

Alarmed by the nearness of those sirens, I got up, too, and hurried out to the porch in my bare feet. July's heat still warmed the porch floor. Stars blazed overhead but darkness lay everywhere around me except for flashing red lights that lit up tall pine trees a quarter-mile to the west and told me that the fire trucks had stopped at a neighbor's house. Not at one of my brothers' and not at the old wood-framed house where I was raised and where Daddy still lived.

Truck keys jingling in his hand, Dwight joined me and looked toward those woods, grim-faced. "Not Mama's house," he said. "Ogburn's place or Landon's, I reckon." Then he was in the truck, roaring down our long driveway. A moment later, my brother Seth's truck cut through our yard to follow closely behind Dwight. Our nephew Reese brought up the rear.

I wanted to join them, but our ten-year-old son was sound asleep and I knew Cal would be alarmed if he woke up and found both of us gone, so I batted at the mosquitoes that whined around my ears and kept watching. Abruptly there was another flare of bright light beyond the trees and a split-second later, I heard the explosion.

I ran back inside for my telephone.

Dwight answered on the first ring. "It's Taylor Ogburn's house," he said tersely. "Did you hear the dynamite? He was blasting out tree stumps last week and must have left a stick in his truck. It was under the carport and it caught fire before they could drag it out."

"Is Taylor okay?" I asked.

"Don't know yet, shug. He's not outside here and if he was in the house..." His voice trailed off.

"Dwight?"

"It's gonna be a total loss, Deb'rah. They got here too late to stop it And the dynamite didn't help."

I heard male voices calling to him.

As Sheriff Poole's chief deputy, he would be needed. "Gotta go," he said. "I'll be home soon as I can."

By now, it was almost two in the morning and I was due in court at nine, so I got back in bed even though I was too worried to sleep.

Taylor Ogburn and my daddy were lifelong neighbors. Back when Daddy was making moonshine, Taylor had been on his payroll as one of his drivers. I've known him since I was a baby. Only last week I had stopped by to give him a jar of jam that I'd made from the peaches he'd given us.

Money-poor but land-rich, Taylor was a crusty old bachelor who, as he aged, became so concerned with climate change that he's tried to do his bit to slow it down. He grows his own fruits and vegetables, composts his kitchen waste, and tries not to buy anything that comes packaged in wrappings that can't be recycled. He owns a twenty-year-old truck but his tractor probably clocks more miles in an average year.

Daddy thinks Taylor's a bit cracked on the subject, but they've been friends too long to let that get in the way and he shares Taylor's attitude toward land. Any spare nickel either of them has ever had goes into buying more of it. "Cause they sure ain't making any new bits," he says, and Taylor always nods agreement.

Between us, Daddy and my brothers and I own around two thousand acres. Taylor must have acquired at least a thousand himself over the years. As Raleigh edges out closer and closer to us, developers keep dangling offers in front of us. Land that sold for a few hundred dollars an acre forty years ago is now bringing two or three thousand. More, if it's near one of the major interstate highways which make commuting to the Research Triangle a relatively easy drive.

It was after three before Dwight returned. I smelled the strong odor of smoke that clung to his skin as he slid into bed beside me.

"Taylor?" I asked.

"Still no sign of him," Dwight said. "Doesn't look good. Donny Turner said he saw blood on the porch when they got there. Lots of blood."

Donny Turner was one of the volunteer firefighters. "We'll have to wait till the ashes cool to be sure he wasn't inside. I went over to Benton's house to see if he or Greg knew where Taylor was. They didn't. Said they didn't anyhow."

Greg and Benton King were Taylor's nephew and his only relatives, the sons of his late sister. I picked up on the tone of Dwight's voice. "Were they lying?"

He shrugged. "Who knows with those two? Both of 'em had had been drinking and swore they hadn't seen Taylor in two or three days. As much blood as Turner says he saw, maybe you'll give me a search warrant for their house?

"You think one of them killed Taylor and set the fire?"

"Well, neither of those boys are ever going to get an award for citizen of the year," he said with such a big yawn that I quit asking questions and let him go to sleep.

He was right about Taylor's nephews, though. As a district court judge, I had dealt with both of them on drunk and disorderly charges. They got into more than their share of fights and they couldn't seem to hold a job for very long. Taylor bailed them out each time, but he always looked grim if their names came up when I visited him. He had loved his sister and I could see how disappointed he was by the way her sons were turning out.

Next morning, after Cal left for school, I rode over to Taylor's with Dwight, who carried in his shirt pocket the search warrant I'd signed. Several of the neighbors were there, including Dwight's mother and my father. Buster

Cavanaugh, our fire marshal was poking through the remains of the house with his staff. Buster's a political appointee and knows squat about the job, but at least he's had the sense to hire some competent assistants. "No sign of a body," he told Dwight.

Daddy had heard about the blood that Donny Turner had seen. "You think somebody killed him and then set the fire to hide it?" he asked Dwight.

"Too soon to tell," Dwight said. "Taylor have any enemies you know about?"

"Not an enemy," said Daddy. "Just those two sorry nephews who keep trying to get some of their inheritance early."

"Inheritance?"

"They're his only kin and they thought Taylor was setting on a gold mine."

"His land?" I asked.

"Yeah. Some developer wanted to buy that eight-acre piece over near that new grocery store. Was offering twelve thousand for it."

"I'm guessing Taylor said no?"

Daddy nodded.

"So now it's Benton and Greg's to sell?"

"I reckon. I told Taylor he ought to make a will, but he kept putting it off. Hoped that one of them boys would stop thinking the land's a piggy bank instead of something worth holding on to and taking care of. He saw Benton throw trash from a Bojangles chicken sandwich out of his truck window and he almost called John Claude to draw up a will right then to leave it all to Greg."

John Claude Lee is my cousin and former law partner.

"But—?"

"But then next day, Greg came out and tried to borrow money to buy some equipment for a lawn service he and Benton were going to start up.

"So he never made a will?"

"Not that I ever heard."

Daddy sighed at the thought of yet another hunk of good farmland turned into cookie-cutter houses for Raleigh commuters.

Dwight's mother was just as gloomy. A retired school principal, she foresaw an influx of new children whose parents would lobby for charter schools as the state moves ever closer to resegregation.

I looked out past the burned remains of Taylor's house to his organic gardens and orchard and the pine woods beyond. As soon as his nephews took title, the woods would probably be timbered and the gardens bulldozed into housing plots. Overhead, a red-shouldered hawk called and I heard its mate call back from the edge of the woods. Taylor had showed me their nest in the top fork of a tall pine. "Third year they've nested there," he said proudly. "Lot of folks don't like chicken hawks, but I keep my chickens penned up and it don't bother me none if they take a few squirrels or field mice."

He loved his birds so much that he had patiently coaxed chickadees and sparrows to eat seeds from his hand every winter. Cal had been thrilled when Taylor poured some sunflower seeds in his hand and two tiny finches came and sat on his fingers to feed. I was really going to miss that kindly old man.

Dwight dropped me back at the house and went to search Greg and Benton King's house. I took a quick shower, then headed into Dobbs for court.

"Any luck?" I asked Dwight that afternoon.

"Yep. Benton was burning trash when we got there. We were able to fish out a pair of white sneakers with drops of blood on the toes and more blood in the treads where he could have walked though what was on the porch."

"He say how he got the blood?"

"Swore he'd been in a fight at the Rooster Bar last week and bloodied some guy's nose. Couldn't remember who the guy was and the bartenders didn't remember the fight. Benton's sneakers weren't all though. One of my men found a T-shirt in the laundry hamper with a smear of blood on the front. Greg admitted it was his. Said when he was in Dobbs for the Fourth of July parade, he saw a child fall and scrape its knee. He picked the kid up and carried it back to its mother. Never saw either of them before and has no idea who they are."

Two weeks later, with yet no clear sign as to what had happened to Taylor, his nephews weren't wasting any time. They told everyone who would listen that some unknown killer must have stabbed Taylor and they immediately petitioned the court to have him declared dead so that his estate could be settled.

"What about that bloody T-shirt and Benton's sneaker?" I asked Dwight.

"Benton says he still doesn't remember who he fought with."

"But you sent that sneaker to the lab. Didn't they analyze the blood for DNA? Wasn't it Taylor's?"

"DNA's a great tool," Dwight said, "as long as you have something you can compare it to. We've got nothing. The fire burned up every trace of Taylor. The porch, his truck, the tractor. If we could've saved the truck, it might've had some something on the headrest or a cup in the holder. That would have been enough, but the truck was fried when that dynamite exploded. Hell, Deb'rah! We don't even know his blood type. He was never in the hospital. Barely ever saw a doctor. For an eighty-year-old man, he was healthy as a horse."

"And the blood on Greg's shirt?"

Dwight shrugged. "A kid he never saw before and hasn't seen since? The lab says that the blood on Benton's sneaker is probably from someone related to him, but without a documented sample, there's no way to say that the relative was Taylor. If Benton killed him, I'm afraid he's going to get away with it."

On that discouraging note, the Sheriff's department redoubled their search of nearby woods and ponds, trying to find Taylor's body. They even borrowed a cadaver dog from the SBI. Nothing. Hope glimmered when someone spotted several buzzards circling above a cornfield, but that proved to be a dead deer.

"One hair," said Terry White, an SBI friend who shared Dwight's frustration. "One damn drop of dried saliva."

But the fire had destroyed all the possibilities we could think of.

A few days later, we were having drinks on the back porch when Daddy stopped by and joined us. Most songbirds seem to disappear in the middle of the day and then get active in the early afternoon. With a flurry of bright yellow feathers, a gold finch lit on a zinnia that was going to seed and set about eating the seeds one by one. Bluebirds popped in and out of a birdhouse nailed to a nearby tree, busily feeding their second or third brood of the summer.

"That one of Taylor's boxes?" asked Daddy who recognized his friend's careful workmanship.

"Yes," I said. Taylor had given it to us as a wedding present when Dwight and I were married two years ago.

"He surely did love his bluebirds," Daddy said.

A sweet memory floated to the surface of my brain as I remembered how Taylor had shown me a nestful of chicks only a week ago. Although the birds lay four to six eggs, the usual brood seems to be three. "Looky here," Taylor had said as he opened the box and proudly showed me the crowded nest. "I never had six chicks before."

"His bluebirds!" I exclaimed.

"Huh?" said Dwight.

"We need to go check his nests right now," I said and we piled into Daddy's truck.

A few minutes later, we turned into Taylor's driveway and Daddy pulled up near one of the bluebird boxes nailed to a pear tree out in the orchard. I tapped on the box and after a startled female bird flew out, I removed the nail that kept the door in place and gently pulled out the plastic freezer box that held the nest. Four small featherless chicks, their eyes still unopened, huddled together at the bottom.

"Taylor recycled everything," I reminded Dwight.

"So?"

"Look at this nest," I said.

It was woven of the usual twigs and straws, but to soften it for her brood, the female bird had tucked in weed fuzz and long strands of white hair. "Taylor said he always cleaned his hairbrushes out in the yard," I said. "He liked to leave his hair where the birds could find it for their nests. I'll bet at least some of these have follicles."

Dwight immediately pulled out a plastic evidence bag and transferred several strands of Taylor's white hair from the nest. "I'll need your sworn affidavit that this is his hair," he said.

"You got it," I told him.

Benton King was arrested two days later when a perfect DNA match came back for the blood on his sneaker. It was another two days before he took the D.A.'s deal and confessed to stabbing his uncle and dumping his body in an old abandoned well. As we suspected, money was the motive, but of course, he was barred from inheriting and everything went to Greg.

I wish I could say that all's well that ended well, but life's not that pretty. Greg immediately sold Taylor's land to the highest bidder and several hundred houses are already under construction. Loud bulldozers and chainsaws have obliterated Taylor's peaceful orchard, along with all his bird houses. Ironically, Daddy says he's heard they're going to call the development *Bluebird Ridge*. "Too bad there ain't no bluebirds over there anymore," he says.

— *Ellery Queen Mystery Magazine, January/February 2020*

This story takes place between Killer Market *and* Home Fires.

THE TUESDAY BOOK CLUBS

We all know about the physical traits that can be inherited: hair color, a cleft chin, the shape of a nose; but what about the metaphysical traits? A sense of humor, impulsiveness, maybe even a small streak of larceny? Did one of our great-grandmothers pass these on to Portland or me?

Tuesday, June 11, 1912

This month's hostess: Mrs. Troy Garner. This month's selection: The Anderson Diamonds by Jefferson Comstock.. Our discussion was led by Mrs. Richard Hawkes. Several members felt that the heroine should have realized more quickly who the thief in her household was. Mrs. Calvin Strickland disagreed. She shared with us that two small pieces of her own jewelry are missing. She has let her cook go after the second loss, even though she isn't completely sure that Pearl was the one who took them Mrs. Michael Jones says that she's missing a silver brooch. Mrs. Jones's sister was in need of a cook and has already hired Pearl without Mrs. Strickland's full recommendation.

No old business. New business: three candidates were presented for membership whereupon Mrs. Strickland moved that we adhere to our original limit – no more than 8 members. The motion was put to a vote and passed. Accordingly, all were rejected without prejudice.

"Hey there, honey," Uncle Ash said. Tall and white-haired, he was pouring tea over a glassful of ice cubes when I let myself in the kitchen door after court that afternoon. A second glass of tea sat on the counter. "You're home early. Light calendar?"

"A lot of our speeders and drunk drivers must have gone to the beach last week," I told him. "The Wilmington judges are welcome to my share."

It was such a hot August day that I was glad to take the glass he offered me.

"So how's my second-favorite niece?" he asked with a smile.

His first-favorite is my best friend, Portland Brewer, so I didn't take offense. She's his only blood niece just as I am Aunt Zell's.

"Sorry," I said as I watched him fill a third glass. "I should have realized that you meant this for Aunt Zell. Where is she?"

"In the attic." He handed me the extra glass. "Take this to her if you're going. It's hot as the blazes up there, so please don't let her stay much longer."

Aunt Zell and Uncle Ash's white brick house is only one block off Main Street, a three-minute drive from the courthouse here in Dobbs where I'm a district court judge. It's way too big for two people, but they had planned to fill the extra bedrooms with children. Sadly, their only child died before he was six months old so they had sublimated with two nieces and many, many nephews— my eleven brothers and both of Portland's. Early on, some extra bedrooms had been turned into a suite for his widowed mother; and after her death, they had offered it to me when I finished law school and passed the bar exam.

A formal staircase curves up from the entry hall, but I took the utilitarian back stairs that the live-in help had to use back in the 1890s when the house was first built. Air conditioning was installed about forty years ago, but its cooling power faded the higher I went.

The attic was as hot as Uncle Ash had warned even though Aunt Zell had raised the windows at both gable ends. The cross-ventilation wasn't helping much and her pretty face was flushed as I joined her in front of an old trunk where she was rummaging through rusty black taffeta and yellowed lace.

"Bless you," she said, reaching for the glass of iced tea.

"Bless Uncle Ash," I told her. "He's the one who thinks you need to come back down to where it's cooler. What are you looking for anyhow?"

"One of my grandmother's summer dresses. I thought I remembered... ah! Here it is!" she said triumphantly and pulled from the trunk a long dress made from a pale green cotton fabric that was sprigged with tiny embroidered flowers. "I'll have to buy a new hat, but my green shoes should work just fine."

As she shook out the dress, a small leather-bound notebook fell to the floor. Someone had written *"Minutes of the Felicity Book Club "* on the first page in a beautiful old-fashioned script.

"Bring it along," Aunt Zell said when I showed it to her.

She draped the dress over her free arm, picked up her glass and headed for the door.

The dining room felt downright chilly after the hot attic. Aunt Zell spread the dress on the mahogany table and examined it carefully. "Good. No stains, but as old as it is, I'd better wash it by hand."

If the dress had belonged to her grandmother—my great-grandmother—then it could be at least a hundred years old.

"What's the occasion?" I asked.

"The book club jubilee," she said. "Aren't the Pepyses coming or are y'all too new?"

"Jubilee? What's that?" I had missed my club's last meeting because I was holding court over in Alamance County for a judge who'd had an emergency appendectomy and I hadn't asked for an update because our June book had been a tedious correspondence between two of North Carolina's less illustrious governors.

"The Rosalinds are celebrating their seventy-fifth anniversary in September and they've invited all the other clubs to come dressed as their members would have dressed when their own club first began."

Which explained the hunt for my great-grandmother's summer frock. Of the five book clubs here in Dobbs, Felicity is the oldest and was always considered the most desirable. It was begun about a hundred years ago by eight of the town's most prominent women of the day. Even now there are less than twenty members because each has to be a female descendant of one of the original founders and not all the founders produced female descendants who still live in the area. Aunt Zell keeps trying to get Portland and me to join, but she's an attorney and she's often in court then, too.

Instead, we belong to the Samuel Pepys Book Club, which limits itself to non-fiction diaries, letters or legal histories. Like the other clubs, we meet on the second Tuesday of each month—the second Tuesday night actually, because we all have day jobs. We're each connected to the court one way or another— attorneys, prosecutors, legal secretaries, etc. Unlike the other all-female clubs, several of our members are men. We're on both sides of the political spectrum, which can lead to some pretty hot discussions at times, but so far we haven't come to blows.

While Aunt Zell mended a small tear in that vintage dress, I leafed through the notebook I'd found.

It had belonged to Eleanor Stephenson, my great-grandmother, when she was Felicity's secretary and it covered three years: 1912 to 1915. The first few pages were devoted to the membership roll which she had dutifully checked off each month, with a notation as to whether or not a member's absence was excused.

"They had to bring a note from home?" I asked.

Aunt Zell smiled. "No, but they did have to present a legitimate reason for not attending. We still do. If we give in to age because it's easier to stay home than get out, we soon wouldn't have a functioning club at all."

I was amused to see how the names were listed: *Mrs. James Robertson* and I knew that this is how the roll is still called, not "Mariah Robertson" even though these women have known each other since kindergarten. "Tradition," Aunt Zell says when I tease her about their formality. "It was white gloves and hats back then."

Most of the surnames in that notebook were familiar to me, but as I scanned the roll, one name stood out by its absence. "I don't see a Mrs. Smith," I said. "Wasn't one of Uncle Ash's grandmothers a member?"

"Not in the beginning," Aunt Zell said as she snipped a loose thread. "I don't know all the details, but my own grandmother was downright apologetic when she heard I was going to marry Ash. Mrs. Smith's name was first put up for membership when the club began. My grandmother didn't know her very well at the time, but thought she would be fun. Unfortunately, there was a prominent woman who didn't like her and spoke against letting her in. I gather hard words were exchanged, and Mrs. Smith wasn't invited to join until 1913. It was something of a scandal at the time."

"Over joining a book club?"

"You don't understand, honey. It was such a point of pride for a lot of those ladies that if you weren't a member of one of the clubs, you just didn't stick your nose out the door on a Tuesday afternoon because everyone would know you hadn't been invited to join one."

Several pages near the back of the book held small pictures of the women printed on calling cards. "Cartes de visite," said Aunt Zell when I showed her. She studied the names. "There's my grandmother and that must be Ash's grandmother." She pointed to the last picture. "Mrs. Jefferson Smith."

I'd never seen a picture of Portland's great grandmother, but I could see the strong family resemblance: the same curly dark hair and shining dark eyes that seemed to twinkle with mischief.

December 10, 1912

Hostess, Mrs. Aaron Starling. Book: St. Elmo by Augusta Jane Evans. Discussion led by Mrs. Phillip Barclay, who read us an obituary of Augusta Jane Evans, who died 3 years ago. Various members told of relatives named Edna Earl, whose mothers were captivated by this book and admired the character's erudition and goodness. Mrs. Barclay suggests that the romance between the virtuous and religious Edna Earl and the rich and cynical St. Elmo is a variant of the Cinderella theme in which an humble girl captures the love of a noble prince.

No new business, but Mrs. Hawkes confided that her mother-of-pearl cameo is missing and Mrs. Jones can't find an onyx hatpin that she last remembers using two weeks ago. I myself am missing the silver bracelet my sister gave me for my birthday. Other members say they've mislaid things, too. We all plan to go home and see if any small trinkets are gone from our jewelry boxes. Has a thief targeted our members? "If so," asked Mrs. Jones, "Why take just your bracelet and leave your diamond earrings and nice gold necklace?" Mrs. Jones is Sheriff Mcgee's sister and she will speak to him tonight even though nothing of great value seems to have been taken.

Aunt Zell's brow furrowed when I read her that entry in the book club notes. "I do seem to remember one of our older members telling Mother about a spate of small thefts that went on for several months back then. I don't think they ever found the thief or recovered any of the missing items, but Grandmother must have been mistaken about her silver bracelet because she left it to your mother. Didn't Sue give it to you for Christmas one year?"

"She did," I said. "It's engraved with flowers. I'd forgotten that it was Great-grandmother Stephenson's."

"Lucky she found it," said Aunt Zell. "One woman was so provoked that she fired the best cook she'd ever had and for no reason as it turned out."

"A Mrs. Strickland," I said, reading her that passage from the minutes book. "Would that be someone kin to the Macon Strickland who owns the hardware store?"

"His great-aunt, I should think," said Aunt Zell. "Grandmother told Mother that she tried to hire Pearl back, but Pearl's new employer was paying her quite a bit more and Pearl was still miffed that she'd been suspected of stealing. Pearl Rowland was something of a legend in her time. You know those angel rolls that you and your brothers like so much? That was her recipe."

Just the mention of those rolls made my mouth water. They were light and yeasty yet rich with a buttery flavor to die for. "She invented those rolls?" I said. "That Mrs. Strickland must have been an idiot to fire someone that good."

I turned to the back of the book and found the woman's picture. She wore a high lace collar and pearl drop earrings. Pinched lips and narrowly set eyes. It may have been my imagination but I thought Mrs. Strickland had a sour expression.

Reading that the thefts had been reported made me curious enough to stop by the Sheriff's department after court next day where I went looking for Mayleen Richards. She's the current sheriff's first female officer, but she trained as a programmer and he values her computer skills as much as her gutsy approach to law enforcement. I found her sorting through a stack of old manila file folders and explained what I was looking for.

"A nineteen-twelve robbery report?" She asked. "I've been digitizing these records, but I'm only back to the nineteen-fifties."

She was willing to see what she could find, though, and was soon thumbing through the lower drawer of a battered green file cabinet. "Strickland, did you say? Nineteen-twelve?"

"Mrs. Calvin Strickland. They all went by their husband's names back then."

"Here it is." She opened a stained and frayed folder to scan the three sheets of yellowed paper inside. "Winston McGee was the sheriff back them. Beautiful handwriting." She turned the folder so I could see the clear cursive of Sheriff McGee's notes.

According to those notes, several women reported that they were missing some pieces of jewelry. Nothing of great value, but the complainants were unsettled that it had happened. One sheet held rough sketches of the items as described to the sheriff, each neatly labeled with the owner's name. One sketch was of my great-grandmother's silver bracelet. McGee theorized that since all the victims were members of the Felicity book club, the thefts probably took place on the Tuesday when they were out and their cooks and housekeepers had the afternoon off.

"No suspects and none of these things were ever recovered," Mayleen said. "In January of 1913, Sheriff McGee suggested that the ladies start locking their doors and promised to send out someone to patrol the club members' neighborhoods on the second Tuesdays but the thefts seem to have stopped as suddenly as they'd begun."

"The Felicity club was the only one targeted?" I said. "Do you think a club member was the thief?"

"That would be my guess," Mayleen said. "If they met in each other's houses, then everyone would be familiar with where things were. That roll book you found—was someone frequently absent?"

"Not that I can see. On the other hand, no one seemed to know exactly when their things went missing."

Sheriff McGee's case notes might not have been a help, but there was one more possibility. Out at the farm. Daddy's housekeeper Maidie Holt beamed when I asked her if she'd known a Pearl Rowland. "Miss Pearl? Indeed I did. Ninety-six when she passed about ten years ago, and sharp as carpet tack right up to the end. Why you asking?"

I explained about the book club, the thefts, and how Pearl Rowland had been suspected, then fired.

"Never heard nothing about that," Maidie said, "but no way would Miss Pearl ever take something that didn't belong to her. She was one of the first deaconesses at our church. Tell you who might know—her granddaughter, Alice Bassinger."

"Is that the same Alice who works in the Clerk of Court's office?" I asked.

"If that's in the courthouse," Maidie said. "Her mama died when she was eight and Miss Pearl raised her."

"I know her," I said. "She helped me look up some deeds last fall."

Next morning, I called and arranged to meet Pearl's granddaughter for coffee before I was due in court.

Alice Bassinger had smooth dark brown skin, liquid brown eyes and an interested smile when we met at the coffee shop. We had gotten past the Judge Knott/Ms. Bassinger formalities last fall and were able to pick up where we'd left off. "You said this was about my grandmother?"

"Pearl Rowland, yes," I replied. I read her the passage my great-grandmother had recorded in the Felicity Book Club's minutes and how Mrs. Strickland had reacted to the thefts. "Did she ever say anything about that incident?"

"*Say* anything?" Alice laughed. "Till the day Gramma died, she could get red hot about being accused of taking some dime store jewelry as she called it. That Mrs. Strickland was always finding fault for no reason. But Gramma got the last laugh. Mrs. Strickland apologized and begged her to come back, but her new employer was nicer and paid better money, so no way would Gramma ever work for that woman again."

"There was nothing in Sheriff McGee's records about who the thief was. Did your grandmother suspect anyone?"

Bassinger shook her head. "No, but she thought it was probably somebody who wanted to get back at some of the ladies who might have been ugly to her."

"Ugly, how?"

"Gramma said that sometimes, a lady might ask to join the Felicity club but Mrs. Strickland always voted against adding new members. Gramma said it was because her dining room could only seat ten people when all the other ladies could seat twelve. That embarrassed the daylights out of her. So she was always finding different reasons to say no when the others suggested a new member. Some of those ladies might have taken it personally when they were rejected. Gramma heard part of the discussions when she was serving lunch and a couple of times, she said it could get real contentious. Mrs. Strickland was usually the one who had the worst things to say, so if it got back to the woman in question..."

I nodded. "You said your grandmother called it dime store jewelry?"

"Those ladies were well-to-do," said Alice, "but Gramma thought that the things that were taken were all pretty cheap—silver, not gold and maybe rhinestones and colored glass instead of diamonds and rubies. That's why Sheriff McGee didn't take it very seriously—like somebody was playing a joke on them. Anyhow, it stopped after Mrs. Strickland left the club."

"*What?*"

"You didn't know? Gramma said she got voted out a few months later."

There was no time to flip through the Felicity minutes right then, but as soon as I recessed for lunch, I closed my office door and started skimming my great-grandmother's notes.

March 11, 1913

Hostess, Mrs. Aaron Starling. Book: The Harvester by Gene Stratton-Porter. Discussion led by Mrs. James Robertson. The general consensus is that this book did not live up to the standard set by Freckles, the last Porter book we read. The hero struck some of us as rather smug with his high-minded life of herbs and animals.

Old business: As no thefts have been reported since January, Sheriff McGee will no longer set his deputies to watch our houses.

New business: Mrs. Lawrence Buffkin is confined to her bed with influenza. We voted to send her a fruit basket. Several members have once more suggested that Mrs. Jefferson Smith be invited to join our club. Before Mrs. Calvin Strickland could speak against her again, Mrs. Starling noticed that a topaz ring had fallen from Mrs. Strickland's pocket when she pulled out a handkerchief. Mrs. Barclay immediately claimed it as identical to the one she had reported missing. Mrs. Strickland insists that she had never seen it and had no idea how it got into her pocket. After much discussion, Mrs. Strickland offered her resignation, which was accepted. It was moved and seconded that Mrs. Smith be invited to join us and to be given Mrs. Strickland' status as a founding member.

"*Wow!*" I thought. That must have been one hell of a meeting. Contentious Mrs. Calvin Strickland had resigned after dropping a stolen ring? And "after much discussion," Portland's great-grandmother was invited to join the Felicity Club as if she'd been a founding member from the start? I wondered if Portland knew.

"She wasn't a Felicity from the beginning?" asked Portland when I called her after work that evening. Portland and I have been best friends since kindergarten so I accepted when she invited me to supper.

"Avery's grilling steaks on the terrace," she said. "Why don't you come over and bring that record book?"

An hour later, while her husband charred the edges of our steaks and she put together a salad, I told Portland what I'd learned about the Felicity Club and how her great-grandmother came to be considered a founding member. She was delighted to see Mrs. Smith's picture and amused to hear that the club's membership was originally limited by the size of a member's dining room.

"Pearl Rowland's granddaughter says that this Mrs. Strickland could only seat ten, which is why she wasn't eager to add more members."

"Or maybe she just didn't like my great-grandmother," said Portland.

"Well, if she was like you or your mother—" Avery teased.

"Are you saying we're hard to get along with?" Portland asked indignantly.

"Just opinionated," he said and dodged the cherry tomato she threw at him.

As I started to put the minutes book back in my briefcase, one of the papers Mayleen had copied for me slid out of its folder.

"What's that?" asked Portland.

"Sheriff McGee sketched out the pieces of jewelry that were taken," I said, handing her the paper. "Nothing of much value, according to the minutes my great-grandmother took. Pearl Rowland called it all dime store stuff."

She glanced at the drawings and started to give them back when her eyes widened. "Oh my God, Deborah!"

"What?" I asked.

"That bar pin! It had a cluster of shiny rhinestones on one end. See? And this cameo! Your mother gave us a Valentine box of stuff to play dress up with when we were little, and these things were in it. Remember that dragonfly pin and those dogwood earrings?"

Until then, I'd forgotten all about that red heart-shaped candy box that had held a tangle of costume jewelry, plastic beads and brooches. I was immediately awash in childhood memories of playing dress-up and now that I looked more closely at Sheriff McGee's sketches, I recognized several pieces that we had bedecked ourselves with.

"Where did your mother get them?" Portland asked.

A quick phone call to Aunt Zell answered that question. "It was probably something that was in my grandmother's house when we cleaned it out," she said. "I think Sue took a box of costume jewelry for some craft project she was planning, but she never got around to it so you girls got to play dress-up with it. I have a picture of you two somewhere. Y'all were so cute."

I told Portland what Aunt Zell had said, but I was still puzzled. "So how did my grandmother wind up with all the stolen goods and why didn't she give everything back to their owners?"

Portland was still holding the sketches. "There's that Mrs. Barclay's topaz ring and your mother's silver bracelet."

"Oh, dear Lord!" I said.

"What?" asked Portland.

"Aunt Zell said that my great-grandmother thought yours would be a welcome addition to the book club but that bitchy Mrs. Strickland kept voting against her."

"So?"

"So think how convenient it was that one of the stolen pieces fell out of Mrs. Strickland's pocket."

"Your great-grandmother *planted* it on her?"

"Well, I do have her silver bracelet and nobody else seems to have gotten any of their things back," I said.

"Not too late," said Portland with a wide smile. "The Felicity club members are all descendants of the original members, right?"

"So?"

She laughed. "The jubilee's still a month away. Plenty of time to dig up that old Valentine box and return everything to their rightful owners. Better late than never, Deborah."

First publihed in Ellery Queen Mystery Magazine, February 2020.

About the Author

Margaret Maron is the author of thirty novels and two collections of short stories. Winner of several major American awards for mysteries (Edgar, Agatha, Anthony, Macavity), her works are on the reading lists of various courses in contemporary Southern literature and have been translated into 17 languages. She has served as president of Sisters in Crime, the American Crime Writers League, and Mystery Writers of America.

A native Tar Heel, she still lives on her family's century farm a few miles southeast of Raleigh, the setting for Bootlegger's Daughter, which is numbered among the 100 Favorite Mysteries of the Century as selected by the Independent Mystery Booksellers Association. In 2004, she received the Sir Walter Raleigh Award for best North Carolina novel of the year. In 2008, she was honored with the North Carolina Award for Literature. (The North Carolina Award is the state's highest civilian honor.) In 2013, Mystery Writers of America named her Grand Master, its highest award. In 2015, the Bouchercon World Mystery Convention awarded her with its Lifetime Achievement Award.

CPSIA information can be obtained
at www.ICGtesting.com
Printed in the USA
FSHW010456290420
69732FS